". . . I admire the hard economy of style, the characterizations . . ."

Raymond Chandler

"Good stuff."   <u>**Chicago Tribune**</u>

"Highly successful and realistic."

<u>**Publishers' Weekly**</u>

(Why not try him yourself?)

THE
STAR RUBY
CONTRACT

PHILIP ATLEE

CORONET BOOKS
HODDER FAWCETT LTD

Copyright © 1967 by Fawcett Publications, Inc.

First published by
Fawcett Publications Inc., New York
Coronet Books edition 1969

SBN 340 02376 7

Printed in Great Britain for
Hodder Fawcett Ltd,
St. Paul's House, Warwick Lane,
London, E.C.4
by Hazell Watson & Viney Ltd,
Aylesbury, Bucks

T HE JETLINER CAME out of a blue Pacific infinity and broke its glide path over the runway, which looked like a freeway, abandoned halfway across the harbor. I listened to the clamor of hydraulic systems and felt the trucked wheel assemblies take the weight of the big aircraft. Heat waves came shimmering up past the windows as we rolled with diminishing speed. After more systems had grunted and squealed, we taxied to a halt, but I did not unbuckle my seatbelt until the other passengers were trooping off.

Kai Tak Aerodrome had been improved since the last time I had seen it. The new runway, reclaimed from the harbor by a tremendous amount of fill, was far safer than the old facility, with its dangerous letdown over the hills.

When I stepped out of the plane, the sultry afternoon hit me in the face. Pausing on the ramp, I glanced across Kowloon Peninsula to the incredible green shadows on Victoria Peak. It was wreathed in fog, but between the drifting patches were remembered grandeurs, the faded pastel mansions of the taipans, the narrow roadways, and the summit tram. And beyond them, on the other side, Aberdeen, Repulse Bay, and the wonderful floating restaurants . . .

"Have a nice stay, sir," piped one of the pretty stewardesses, and I nodded and went down the ramp. I had been holding up the show; the trim girls had laughing assignations to keep. Black-uniformed customs and immigration officials with silver insignia were as polite as ever, flipping through my passport and papers.

They said, "Welcome to Hong Kong, Mr. Mallory. In transit, are you? Fine, sir, enjoy your visit . . ."

In half an hour I had recovered my baggage, endured the buffeting tourists, and by a naked show of wealth snared a cab. This was not as easy as it sounds. An unruly mob was milling around before the terminal entrance, chanting and brandishing placards. The demonstrators seemed to be of many nationalities, colors, and ages and had obviously been bit by some dread tarantula. They were waiting to unload their spleen on a U.S. dignitary, and their legends exhorted all Yanks to go home, especially those in Vietnam.

They were strident about it, impeding traffic, but I skirted their dancing madness and found the greedy cab driver. Rode away from the tumultuous terminal building without learning the result of their organized hubbub. It was far too hot for that kind of nonsense, no matter what moral values were involved, and their strange devices couldn't apply to me because I was a Yank who had just left home.

In another twenty minutes I was following a room boy down a spacious corridor in the Peninsula Hotel. After I had tipped him well, he informed me that I couldn't have a bath for two hours, smiled blandly, and withdrew. As I unpacked I was smiling, too (faintly) because some things hadn't changed. There was still a water shortage in Hong Kong after all the years, and the room boy hadn't told me about it until I had tipped him.

The sequence of these events may be the key to Asia. Whisky I could have, however, so I rang the bell and had some.

I was sitting downstairs watching the big lobby bar fill up when somebody clapped me on the shoulder and a deep voice said, "I warned you long ago that you'd keep ramblin' till the wine turned to vinegar—"

"Potts!" I turned to shake hands with Hal Pottschmidt, a bulky Dutchman who could make the most expensive white sharkskin suit look like a hand-me-down. Potts was

6

a former chief pilot of CNAC and CAT and had been flying in the East for nearly thirty years. His sandy, unruly hair was now a graying fright wig, but he hadn't changed much otherwise.

He was with a small mob of Aussies and New Zealanders, and as he introduced me they responded with slightly inebriated candor, their ladies being even more horse-faced than I remembered. They had just come in from the race course at Happy Valley and were surging toward the bar to stoke inner fires before proceeding to dinner. I responded to their good-natured raillery with short answers like "rooster's ass, cobber" and "so *many* descendents of convicts!" Nobody even noticed.

I was invited to join their swinging company but declined, and as they surged by I asked Pottschmidt to come up to my room for a minute before he left for dinner. He winked and went rolling after them, white jacket bunched up on his big shoulders. As I finished my drink, I saw the boisterous group create space at the bar by main force and heard them bellowing at the bartenders.

I was sitting upstairs in the room, going over some frayed linen flight maps of Southeast Asia, when Potts knocked on the door. When I called, he came in, and I fixed him a *burrah-peg* drink of Scotch. Grunting thanks, he dropped into one of the big leather chairs.

"Long time since you've been on the Kowloon ferry, Joe," he said. "Have you missed the town?"

"Certainly. Everybody does. But my name's Mallory, now. Okay?"

"Unhunh . . ." Potts drank half the glass of Scotch and swirled the rest of it. "Charley Farrell, one of my pilots, went back to the States last year to pick up a new plane for us. Plane wasn't quite ready, so he took off for Mexico City. Says he saw you there one midnight, in the Nicte Ha Bar, with the most beautiful Negro girl in the world. Had bright red hair, yet, Charley says."

A tic hit me over the right eye, as if someone had yanked out a wild hair with a two-inch root. "I have some business in Mexico, once in a while," I said, pressing at

7

the throbbing place. *He was talking about Jannina, the fine blackbird who hadn't come home at all. And never would . . .*

Potts was chuckling. He finished the drink and held the glass toward me. "Everybody in the world flies through Hong Kong, Joe," he said. "Sooner or later . . . And we hear that your business is extensive . . ."

I took the glass and was turning away toward the bar when he added, "Matter of fact, we hear that you must be the biggest spook—"

Freezing, with my back to him, I whipped my fingers in a short arc across my throat. It was the old signal for "aircraft correctly parked, cut your engines," and Potts picked it up smoothly.

". . . reports from Cairo, Barcelona, so I figured you were in some kind of import business . . ."

"That's right," I said, and took him another glass of Scotch.

He cradled the glass in his big, weathered hands. The hail-fellow, jollytime attitude was gone, and he waited quietly. I fixed myself another drink and went back to sit opposite him.

"I want some news circulated, Potts," I said. "I'm going back into Burma in a few days to take over their civil aviation operation. Air Burma, the transport services, everything. And I'm interested in hiring pilots. European, Anzac, or Asiatic—anybody with some time, a multiengine license, and an instrument card. They get paid a flat three thousand a month up to one hundred twenty-five hours, fifty dollars an hour after that. Expenses and three months guarantee . . ."

Pottschmidt's eyes were narrowed, deep in wind wrinkles. "You did that before. Seventeen years ago. Only then you were flying military charter, too . . ."

"That's right. This time I won't control military aircraft."

Potts sipped his drink slowly because he was faced with something he didn't understand. For two and a half decades he had been paying the cumshaw and taking the shake in the Orient, after coming in for Claire Chennault on a passport that said "farmer," and now he wanted some *bona fides*.

"I think you're lying, Joe," he said. "In forty-nine you went in and gutted the Burmese treasury of every dollar, Swiss franc, and pound sterling in it, at the highest charter price ever paid in aviation history. The country was newly independent then, and shaky, but it ain't that way now. General Ne Win is a bulldog, and Burma's been closed airtight to Americans for several years . . ."

I got up and went to the teakwood bench at the end of the bed, unzipped my map case, and returned to toss the contract in his lap. He folded back the long top sheet of pale green, with the rampant golden lions and the Great Seal of the Government of The Union of Burma on it, and read through the document slowly. Glanced up at me, and read it again.

"This should make you a popular man," said Pott-schmidt. "How long will you be taking applications here?"

"Four days."

He shook his head and handed me back the contract, signed by General Ne Win, dictator of Burma. The document hired me as Managing Director of all Burmese flight services, with full authority to hire and discharge all personnel.

"Will you see that the news gets around, Potts? Beginning tonight? I mean to Bangkok, Calcutta, Karachi, Singapore, Melbourne, Sydney, and all way stations . . ."

"Right." He hesitated. "At the price, Joe, some of these jokers might peel off regular airline jobs, and some of them have families here and there."

"I won't take that kind."

"Good." He belted down the rest of his drink and stood up. "I'd better catch up with those digger friends of mine . . . Don't know why, though. I invariably have to whip one of the bastards before dawn, or run like a coward . . ."

I knew what he meant. Australians are what Yanks were fifty years ago; they are not rich enough yet to be neurotic, but they're working on it. In the meantime, they just tee off on the nearest hostile object.

Potts stood fidgeting with his glass. He was half-drunk

and ready to leave, but he couldn't figure out what to do with the glass. That was strange, because his deft touch as a navigator was legendary. Celestial contact, anyway. But among the groundlings he kept pawing at his disordered hair and wrenching his clothes out of shape in aimless indecision.

The seamed face was somber, and the keen eyes steady on me. "I thank you for the drinks, but I'm afraid you've moved slightly out of my sphere."

"Oh?"

"Yes. Burma's closed so tight that Ne Win's even ordered the few remaining missionaries out by the end of the year. People who've lived there sixty, seventy years. Yet he seems to have given you another key to their treasury."

"That's right."

"Okay." Potts held up his big hands in surrender and lumbered toward the door. He looked like a glistening-white, untidy bear.

"I need something else, Potts," I added, and he stopped with one hand on the door knob. "I need a perfumed quiff. A Eurasian girl under twenty, beautiful and with the morals of an alley cat. Educated. Someone who will hang steady, for enough money, as long as I want her."

The big man facing the door didn't move, and the air conditioning hummed. There was something else in the room, too—a queer emotional electricity.

"You had that once before," Pottschmidt said, and threw his head like a gaffed fish. "Someone like Ugette?"

"Just like that," I said.

He nodded. "You've always had the best of it, haven't you, you dirty bastard?" he asked quietly. Since he didn't use profanity often, I knew he was listening closely.

Pottschmidt had never married. He was a drinker and a party-type fellow and, in spite of looking like a used-clothes hamper, had been attractive to women and known a lot of them. A long time ago he had found a fifteen-year-old girl named Ugette dancing in a joint on Bubbling

Well Road, in Shanghai. A young Venus with black nipples, just out of Hanoi.

Tar-brush, sure, but with an incredible figure and a classic face. So he had shacked up with her, after paying $17,000 key money for an elaborate Calcutta apartment. Then one bright summer day I had played tennis with them, and a week later Ugette had moved in with me, in an apartment for which *I* had paid plenty of key money. We had been happy for a year, and I had even taught her to shave her armpits before I left Asia in disgust at the tactics of Chancre Jack's government.

A pilot named Nash had inherited her, and they had stayed together until I returned a few years later to run air operations in Burma, which was finally free of English rule. Ugette had been killed by a Karen grenade just before I left Burma. Potts had been on the periphery of these events, but not near me.

Her accidental death had been, as the English say, deeply regretted by all ranks. But she was gone now, and she had never been anything but an attractive object, like a Playboy bunny. More available, of course, but still, dead . . .

"I'll try to find a suitable replacement," said Pottschmidt heavily. "One to fit your high position. But don't leave the replacement in Burma, too."

"We take these chances, Potts," I said. "And I know you'll do your best because we are blood brothers in the Seonee Wolf Pack. In the locust years when I was a scared young copilot checking out on four-engine equipment, you used to whipsaw me brutally. And then, one dim monsoon afternoon, at the end of the Kunming runway, I hauled your charred ass out of a plane that had crashed on takeoff."

"Yes," said Pottschmidt, "there's always that. I'll have some candidates drop by in the witching hours. Now would it be all right if I got a breath of fresh air?"

"Certainly," I said. "Thanks for dropping by."

T WO HOURS LATER I was bent over the desk again, concentrating on strip maps of the Shan States, when a tap came on the door. I reached for my robe, and went to open it. A young Eurasian girl in a tailored suit was standing in the hall, with some kind of briefcase under her arm, and she asked if I was Captain Mallory.

"Yes," I said, and motioned her in and to a chair. She was tall, and her ebony hair was teased high, combed full in back. The straight lines of the severely tailored suit could not conceal her figure, and her long legs were admirable. While I sat waiting, she rummaged in the briefcase and handed me several papers.

One of them was a certificate of graduation from the Academy of St. Cecilia, another to show that she had completed a secretarial course at Lindsay's Business School, Hong Kong, and the third was her Hong Kong police registration, with a thumbnail picture affixed in the upper right corner.

"Captain Pottschmidt sent you?" I asked.

"Yes, sir."

"You know, then, that the job involves going to Burma for several months?"

"Yes, he told me that."

I gave her back the papers. "I don't have much correspondence. Mostly, I require a traveling companion— one who can do this or that, immediately, when I point. Somebody who won't argue, or foul up."

"I understand," she answered.

"Good. Are you a virgin?"

"No."

"Would you like a drink of champagne?"

"Always and forever," said the dark-eyed girl, clapping her hands. "Whatever hour."

"This," I said, pressing the service button, "is whatever hour, and I often have champagne when it comes around."

When I thumbed the cork out of the first bottle of Bollinger '59 Brut, she watched it hit the ceiling and clapped her hands in delight again. The hands were long and shapely, and had dark half-moons in the nails. We chatted idly through the first bottle, and she seemed to know her way around Hong Kong. She had worked for six months in an import-export house in Seoul, had left there because of the cold, but had liked their pickled *kimchi*. She could do the American dances, she said, Frug and Watusi and the rest, but was uncertain about the thigh-length dresses from London. In her opinion, the Cheong-sam gowns of the Orient could show as much, and you could still sit down in them.

Just table talk . . .

After we had opened the second bottle, I asked her to dance for me. She got up and went thrusting through a passable imitation of the frenetic idiots locked in smoky New York caves. Since she did it without any music, I was interested.

"Solange," I said, "the job I have will keep you away from home for a while. You will live well, but there may be danger, and, when I have problems, I am sometimes rough as a cob."

The girl had fallen back in her chair, laughing, and there was a film of perspiration on her upper lip. "Cob? What is it? I am not so rough as that, am I? I know I cannot dance like my sister, but she trained for many years . . ."

What with whisky in the early afternoon, and champagne on top of it, I seemed to have missed a key remark. "What in the hell has your sister got to do with it?" I asked, and Solange straightened up, wide-eyed.

"I thought Captain Pottschmidt told you. I am the sister of Ugette."

"Are you, now?" I asked.

"Yes. It was always a great thing when her letters about you came to our home in Hanoi."

"She didn't tell me," I said. "Neither did Potts."

"Not so? Oh, yes. And there are two sisters younger than I still there."

I considered this information at some length, and poured her another glass of champagne. She took it like Pepsi-Cola, and I went to the bathroom. When I got back, she was curled up in the big chair again, and had unbuttoned the jacket of her tailored suit.

"Solange," I said, "you have two choices. Either take your convent diploma and go home, or go into the bathroom and have a good wash. All over, and then get into bed."

"I'll bathe," said the tall girl cheerfully, and whirled up out of her chair. I had a glimpse of shapely legs as she turned, and then she was in the bathroom, trying knobs and humming in French.

Soldier, I thought wryly, *this is your night for being reminded of old loves* . . . Potts had done it inadvertently about Jannina, dead in Mexico, and now this girl, a sister of the dark Venus who had been killed in Rangoon.

I hadn't known Pottschmidt was so hung up on Ugette. Christ, in those Shanghai days we were all going full throttle and changed girls like we changed flying jobs. That didn't alter the fact that sending her younger sister to see me *hadn't* been inadvertent.

Then I listened to the happy splashings in the bathtub, and wondered how much wood could a woodchuck chuck? Perhaps this one would be an immortal love, too. Couldn't tell, certainly, until we tried . . .

For the next half hour, while I sipped champagne, Solange splashed and dawdled about and then came back in. A dusky nymph with her damp hair swathed in a towel turban. Still humming, she went sliding under the mosquito netting and into the bed.

I poured what was left of the champagne into two glasses, and she saw the problem and came out to furl the netting. She was beautifully coordinated, the long legs scissoring swiftly. Scrubbed face intent, she took her glass and inched back against the bolster.

Somehow, she had kept the towel turban intact and surveyed me, sipping at her drink. A most aristocratic picture, too, until she hiccuped and spilled most of the champagne between her dark breasts. Laughing, I sat on the edge of the bed.

"Do you think, Captain Mallory," she asked, "that my breasts are too small?"

"Entirely adequate."

"Is it a fact?" She patted the bolster with her free hand, and I stretched out beside her. "I worry about it, you know. Even when I was in the nunnery school, all the girls said that men from the States like enormous breasts. The bigger they were, the more love, you see."

"Not true at all," I said, drained my glass, and tossed it out on the thick carpet. It bounced from rim to base and came to rest on its side. Another glass came over my shoulder, turned twice, and rolled over beside mine. Solange giggled, leaned over me, and began tracing across my chest with a light forefinger.

"But I *read* about it in American magazines," she insisted. "They even tell how some women are having a substance pumped into them—"

"Solange, *cherie*," I sighed, and caressed her ebony hair. Freed from the towel turban, it went far down the sweet curve of her back. "It is being done by some strippers and cabaret performers. One girl in San Francisco had her tit size inflated from thirty-four to forty-three, but the method is not medically approved and may have dangerous side effects."

The dark eyes were fixed on me. "And mine are all right?" she asked again.

"They fit your body wonderfully well," I assured her, and the full lips brushed my ear.

"Okay. How do they do it exactly?"

I turned toward her. "The doctor takes this syringe of silicone fluid, and injects it here. No, not quite, raise your arm a little bit . . . Yes, that's better."

It was, too.

15

An hour later, Solange was sleeping soundly and the towel turban had slipped down over her naked hip. She had said nothing about going home, or how much she was to be paid to work for a man with no correspondence, or anything else. She was just asleep, dimly outlined in the big bed.

I was sitting across the room, studying the flight maps again. I did that for several hours, moving only when she sighed deeply in her sleep. Then I went back to the bed and looked down at her. She was very womanly and defenseless in her sleep.

After checking her, I went back to the shaded desk light and the maps. Soon, with Pottschmidt spreading the word, a weird parade would begin.

A whole troop of American, English, and Anzac pilots—seedy gentlemen and all at liberty—would begin flocking toward me. There would be, too, a few ex-Luftwaffe types, trying not to click their heels because they needed a job so badly, and the usual number of bright Chinese who had flown copilot for thousands of hours. But had never made captain because they couldn't remember to put the gear down when landing . . .

All the one-time heroes and freaks and geeks and opium jockeys who had stayed too long and seen the white ikons smashed. Now they were shabby con-guy pilots who just happened to get caught with narcotics stashed in the folds of their authentic wall-hangings. Ex-bird-colonels who had gone back Stateside, flown elevators for a while, and returned to find that an eagle is just a chicken and a chicken is just a bird.

Yes, I was thinking grimly, staring at the frayed maps with forgotten thunders rolling in my head, that's the kind of crew I need on this one. And when they hear that Gentleman Joe is flinging money around, like old times, they'll come drifting out of temporary dodges to sniff the bait. Among them, after I had weeded out the alcoholics and hype and pipe types, I'd find the crew I needed . . .

W HEN I AWAKENED the next morning, just before
ten, Solange was gone. But she had left a faint depression
on the bed and a trace of cheap perfume on the bolster.
My eyes adjusted; I blinked at the mosquito netting which
enclosed me. The phone began ringing, and I viewed it
with distaste. People continue to give me the word on the
beauties of the world in the morning, and I have tried to
see it but failed.

Perhaps it is because of my odd occupation, but I can
sleep until far past noon, when not actively engaged, and
find the world not much changed when I awaken. The
Hong Kong sandman—or perhaps it was just the champagne—had sprinkled some gravel in my eyelashes.
Knuckling at it, I went to the phone. Not hurriedly,
because people who mean it will keep ringing.

"Mr. Mallory?" inquired a jocose voice.

"Speaking," I said.

"This is Frank Meyers." The voice was almost lilting.
"I had a letter from Artie, and he asked me to look after
you."

"Very nice of you, but I don't need—" Frank Meyers
was the agency station chief in Hong Kong, and I needed
his help like I needed the Stalin Peace Prize.

". . . said you were on a tight schedule," he went on
with bland euphoria, "but I thought we might have a
drink, chin-chin, and see if I could help you."

"I don't think so," I said.

There was a short silence on the line, and he spoke
again. The blandness was gone. "Promised Artie, you
know. We could certainly squeeze in a drink, at least."

"Where, and when?" I asked. I knew the bastard had

been in Hong Kong so long, abetting ineffectual myths like West Wind and the proposed invasion from Formosa, that it was a real waste of time, but I might as well let him throw his weight around. As it turned out, I underestimated Frank.

He gave me an address on the Peak, and said three that afternoon could fit his schedule. I said I would be there, and hung up. Meyers was in the set-mentality group of the Chiang Kai-Shek lobby. With overaged troops, dominating a Formosa that hated his guts, the Generalissimo was still going to attack 700 million mainland Chinese, although none of them wanted him back.

But Meyers knew, and he was going to follow triumphant Chiang right back into Peking. Now he wanted to talk to me in one of the scores of "safe houses" he kept in Hong Kong, whispering about a hope that never was.

I had a leisurely lunch in the Peninsula dining room, and was interrupted by seven pilot applicants. I noted their credentials on the back of the menu, and said they would hear from me. Knowing that none of them was what I needed. At three o'clock I was stepping out of a cab before a faded pink mansion high up on Victoria Peak. A servant answered the door before I could press the bell and bowed me along a long hall, through a drawing room, and out onto an awninged terrace.

Meyers was waiting. He was a chunky, frog-faced man wearing a tailored suit of black Persian mohair that would have cost $300 in the States.

"Good to see you," he said, and shook my hand with more warmth than the occasion deserved. "Sit down, amigo. Got all the makins."

The "makins" was a pitcher of martinis resting in a silver salver filled with ice. I accepted a chilled glass filled with this fluid, and sank into one of the rattan couches. At the edge of the terrace there was a sheer drop of several hundred feet onto one of the narrow, winding roads. I sipped the chilled drink and gazed past Meyers at the arching fronds and profusion of tropic flowers.

"Going into Burma again, are you?" he said expansively, lifting one leg over the edge of his couch. "Sounds great! We haven't been able to get any of our people in there for three years. That Ne Win is a tough bastard."

"Your people are still not in," I said. "Just me, under contract."

"Oh look, now," Meyers said easily, "I've got three boys, all of them Burmese. They can be useful, won't bother you at all."

"No," I said.

He shrugged inside his expensive suit; worried his shaven jowls. "Now man, wait . . ."

"You wait," I said. "I work under contract on black assignments only, and there is a clause in the contract that says you, and people like you, are to be consulted at my pleasure. Not yours. Stay out of my business."

Meyers blinked at the tips of the banyan trees; he rolled his eyes in his froggy face, and lay back. "I had an eyes-only message on you, Gall, and the report is that you have caused trouble in every station you entered. I don't intend for that to happen here."

"It won't." I said, "because I'm in transit. I'll be gone in a few days."

Something, somewhere, had gone badly wrong. For this genial fop to know about my assignment, and to be racking me up, meant the crossing of wires which should have automatically short-circuited. Meyers, like most station chiefs, was as well known as the local chief of police.

"Not good enough," he announced languidly, staring at the blue sky over Hong Kong. "I control the Asia action, and I'm not going to have any jailbird romping through and stirring things up."

"Oh?" I asked. The gloves were off.

"That's right. I have the whole make on you, hard boy. Did some hump duty, quit when the going was rough. Marine hero of sorts, a turn in ordinary espionage, and now you only handle contract work. That right?"

"Yes," I said, putting my drink on the table.

"We also know," Meyers said, "that you served as managing director of a charter airline in Burma, went back home and found your wife in bed with another guy.

19

The record says that you clubbed both of them to death with a portable radio."

"True," I said. "Some of those little radios have great hand-holds on them."

"My God!" said Meyers. "You admit it!"

I got up, took him by the wrist and ankle, and held him over the edge of the terrace, bracing my forearms on the ornamented iron railings. Objects began falling out of the pockets of his expensive suit, and his head was swiveling around wildly. He grabbed for the railing, but I leaned out farther, and he didn't make it.

"It's not considered polite to talk about it," I said. He was still thrashing around, and I flipped him like wet-wash. "Understand?"

"Yes, yes!" he screamed in terror. I shook him again as he dangled over the green-fronded abyss, then jerked him back up and slammed him against the inside wall of the terrace.

"You stupid prick," I said, "I'll say it once. Play golf. Get drunk and act like a Cleveland Buddha. Dream your Formosan dreams . . . If you bother me again, I'll snap your spine."

I walked back through the safe house and found the cab still waiting, although I hadn't mentioned it to the driver. I don't know why he was still waiting. Maybe he subscribed to the Kiplinger newsletter; it's a hell of a lot more accurate than most of our routine intelligence reports. As we rolled down off the Peak, I dried my hands with my handkerchief. They were sweating, because we had nearly lost one of our best station chiefs.

The bright cabbie noticed that my hands were shaking and asked me why. I told him that I had a long history of breakbone fever, and sometimes it just came on me.

TWO WEEKS BEFORE all this laying-on of hands, I had been on a live-pigeon shoot in the Arkansas Ozarks, and the assignment reached me there. This shooting event, while illegal, was patronized by many hill marksmen (including the sheriff of the county), and some of them used heirloom rifles with remarkable success. In addition, because the shoot was held on the estate of a Chicago industrialist, we always had a scattering of guests from all over the country.

On the final day of the event a Kansas City lawyer walked over beside my Rover while I was loading gun cases in it. He was a florid man whom I had met a couple of times, in other years, at the same shoot, but we had never had any contact beyond that. I had, as a matter of fact, avoided him because, like most of the other tycoons, he viewed the shoot as an opportunity to drink as much white moonshine whiskey as possible. And I suppose it made sense to him. For those few days, in a womanless society, he could get completely loaded and tell jokes and drop his suspenders below his butt when he felt like it.

When this sporting type came toward me behind his juridical belly, caparisoned in hundreds of dollars worth of shooting gear, I smiled with reservation.

" 'at was a beautiful triple you picked off there, Joe," he said. "Good a delayed swing shot as I ever saw."

"Thanks," I said.

"No kidding." He handed me a heavy catalog, and I saw that it was *Stoeger's*. "You remember that new ballistics thing we were talking about? No casing, but the slug still manages to come out of the barrel? The one they're working on now, at the Daisy plant in Rogers?"

I said "yes," although we had never discussed this new

ballistics concept, or anything else. I had only nodded at him when we were being introduced. Now he was leaning against the back end of my custom coupe, wafting out fumes of raw whiskey, and I was hoping that his elaborate shooting jacket, courtesy of Abercrombie & Fitch, wouldn't scar the paint job.

I knew what he was talking about. It was a new concept in firepower. Slug and shell were integrated and there was nothing to be ejected after firing. Everything came out of the end of the barrel and went for the target. The Daisy Air Rifle Company, strangely enough, had the U.S. rights, and the Belgian inventor was working in their Arkansas plant.

I started to open the catalog, but my drunken friend leaned down, said quietly, "When you get home," and pinned my hands. He didn't sound a bit drunk, so I put the heavy catalog in the back end of the car, with my gun cases. Then I straightened and glanced around at the activity on the grassy hillside. Men preparing to depart in Cadillacs, Continentals, and ancient jalopies belching smoke. Nobody seemed to be watching us.

I thanked him, shook hands, and drove down to the highway. When I was thirty miles away from the hilltop estate, I doubled back along a hard-surfaced farm access road, stopped, and reached back for the gun catalog. The inside of it was hollowed out, and the blue-covered assignment instructions were neatly contained inside.

I did not open them, only memorized the serial numbers on the cover and drove fifty miles across a state line to a medium-sized town. There, from a phone booth at the edge of a filling station driveway, I called the Washington, D.C. number, station to station, and when I got an answering click and ping, gave my code word. There was another ping, and I articulated clearly the numbers which appeared on the cover of the assignment instructions.

There was another spaced ping, a ten-second wait, and the receiver crackled in my ear. "Yes," it said, and I hung up the receiver and drove another hundred and ten miles to my home, which was on a higher and even more remote

Ozark hill than the one on which the pigeon-shoot had been held.

My garage was in a hillside cave, and from it I had to walk a hundred yards up to the front gate, which was ten feet high and electrified. On both sides of the gate chainlike fences of the same height went stretching away around the hillside, which was covered by a ninety-foot stand of pines through which breezes were always sighing or raging.

Standing before the high gate, I said the three words, and it swung open noiselessly. When I had passed through, and gone up the flagged walkway toward the enormous clapboard castle, the gates latched behind me. A few lights behind narrow, stained glass windows colored the lowering dusk, and when I stepped up on the columned porch, some of the boards groaned.

They had a right to. The house was nearly a hundred years old, and I had spent several years restoring it but hadn't finished the job. I unlocked the massive front door and went inside. Walked down the wide hallway switching on the pale radiance of chandeliers. No answering sound came, no welcoming voice, because I had lived in the house alone for several years.

I snapped on the drawing room lights and turned them to dim with the rheostat. In the butler's pantry I got ice, a bottle of Black Daniel's, and a pitcher of cold spring water. I took them back to the big leather seat beside the fireplace and tossed a match at the logs in the fireplace. The logs ignited because they were covered with kerosene-soaked sawdust.

The log sections blazed, warming my face, and I had a double Daniel's and read the instructions. They were astonishing, so I went over them three times and consigned them to the flames.

While the blue-jacketed document curled to flame and ashes I had another dollop of the good bourbon. The flames mounted and bathed my reflective face with warmth. After staring into the flames for another quarter

23

hour, I went down the narrow stairwell to the basement.

Another switch before I walked out onto the terrace, and indirect lights flashed on back of the pine grove. Illumined the long pool fed by the thirty-foot waterfall, and beyond, fell in pale radiance around the life-sized Buddha figure meditating before a cluster of black bamboos.

I walked across the arching bridge, mandarin red by day but now black under artificial light, and ducked under the icy waterfall spray of the grotto beyond. Inside was a sauna hut, and I lighted the gas jets inside it, under the wrought iron basket of stones.

When the igneous stones were beginning to glow, I caught a bucket of water from the fall and quenched them. A billowing tower of steam arose, and I stripped and sat on the highest shelf for twenty minutes. That was enough. With sweat cascading down my ears and off my chest, I scrubbed myself with rough salt and a loofah.

Outside the sauna hut, I unhooked the two-inch hawser rope and swung out through the icy waterfall. Dropped into the dark pool. Shocking! Thrashing out, I found a fresh towel in the base of the Japanese lantern, and dried myself going back to the house.

For the next hour I sat beside the flickering logs and rechecked the assignment from memory. This time I was going to Burma, a place I had been before but not for a long time. I had recognized a great many of the people mentioned in the nine-page sheaf of instructions, and wondered how many of them I would encounter.

Such odd deliveries and assignments were nothing new to me because I am a contract counterintelligence agent and have been for several years. The name on my rural-route postal box, high on this remote Ozark hill, reads "J. L. (for Joseph Liam) Gall," but you will not find that name in any U.S. census, on any public school or university roll, or anywhere else.

When I was fifteen, a pilot named Lee Miles (he won the Thompson Trophy Race twice) taught me how to get a Cub on and off the ground. Then he taught me to wring it out while upstairs. That kind of interest will keep you out of the poolroom, but you don't get to church very often, either. In spite of estimable country-club-type parents, I was flying the Himalayan route early in War Deuce, at age eighteen, for the China National Airline. And God knows why, but I survived that murderous shuttle for nearly three years.

When it became apparent that the Kuomintang Government was corrupt, and that most of the stuff we flew into China was being sold to the Japanese Army or to Chinese merchants for private sale, I gave the job back to them and enlisted in the Marine Corps. That goddamned near got me killed, too, but fate seems to favor cuckoos. Instead, I took a bad ankle hit at Iwo Shima.

A long time in several hospitals followed, during which I fought off surgeons who wanted to amputate the left foot. While they were still arguing, I splinted the poor member with two palate depressors and some tape and limped away at high speed. After nearly a year of physiotherapy, on my own, I regained efficient if limited use of the foot and got married.

My wife was a beautiful girl, could play Malaguena on the piano, and had a tendency to topple into bed with strangers. We had one very nasty patch, and after the grand jury no-billed me, I gave up my plans to enter law school and decided to be a permanent drunk and horse-player. That involved considerable migration, and I might still have been at it if I hadn't received an unusual cablegram in Hot Springs, Arkansas.

The cable was from Lloyd Varley, a pilot I had known on the China route. It said that if I was free to leave immediately, Varley wanted me to proceed Hong Kong soonest to be briefed on handling flight operations for his charter airline in Burma. And if my answer was yes, on receipt of that cabled information he would cable me $5,000 immediately.

I got drunk four more times, with friends, just on the strength of that cablegram.

He did send the check, however, and in three days I was in Hong Kong. I ran a tight and highly profitable operation in Burma. Our planes were carrying troops and ammunition, and in the few months it lasted I earned Varley over a million dollars, but reinjured my ankle in a crash landing and had to go back into the veteran's hospital in Klamath Falls.

While I was enduring further surgery, a little man named Howard Shale recruited me as an intelligence agent, and I spent several years roaming the globe and acting as one of Uncle Sam's demented Boy Scouts. That was natural, because this country had never had any intelligence systems before.

Then came Fidel. Everything seems to date from Fidel. I had been with him, under orders from the agency, in the Oriente hills, and he looked good there. Later, before the Bay of Pigs, I told an august conclave of my betters that we didn't have a whore's chance in church with the invasion, and so I went down the drain.

Half pay, then no pay, and off the Civil Service list. With little more than my Marine Corps disability pension, I removed to the Ozark region, bought the century-old, dilapidated clapboard castle on a hill, and set about restoring it. Then one day the director of the agency's action division came to see me with an assignment. They needed a hammer, and he had remembered that I was not much on pilfering from files or wastebaskets, but had changed conditions, physically, in a few places.

My first few assignments, always on this contract basis, took me to the Caribbean, the Canary Islands, Spain, Sweden, France, Tahiti, Mexico, and Peru. I did well enough on them, I suppose, because I either solved or short-circuited the problems involved, and am currently under death sentence (in absentia) in Spain and Tahiti. The Soviet Union has been kind enough to plant stories in Western European publications that I am a contract murderer with the hidden rank of Brigadier General, and that I have wantonly slaughtered nineteen people.

These reports are always inflated.

There are, of course, defects in a job like mine. Everytime I leave my house, on which I have worked long and hard, I have to shut it down entirely. On the

26

supposition that I won't be coming back. That means closing my greenhouse in the basement, with its forests of tiny trees, and cutting the air conditioning off my mushroom beds. Writing letters to close out bank accounts, and instructing my lawyer.

Such preparations for the Burma trip took another hour, and then I walked away from the gingerbread mansion again. It loomed dead with no light behind its stained glass windows, but I never looked back. You can't afford roots, or root-convictions, in my business. I threw my bag and map case in the back of the Rover coupe, and drove down the hill through the stand of sighing pines, toward Hong Kong . . .

FOUR DAYS AFTER I had flown into Hong Kong I led a party of six back to Kai Tak Aerodrome, and we caught the Cathay-Pacific flight to Rangoon. The girl, Solange, was wearing her ebony hair high, and her black Cheongsam sheath caused a brief moment of awed inspection as we crossed the terminal. The plane took off on schedule, and when we were at cruising altitude, I opened my map case and inspected all the visas, customs declarations, and international health cards for the group. I had arranged for them so hurriedly that I wanted to be sure nothing was missing.

Solange got up and collected passports from the four pilots I had hired, and I checked them against the special visas. When I was fairly sure we wouldn't foul up in customs and immigration at Mingaladon Aerodrome, in Rangoon, I had her return the passports and leaned back with my eyes closed, listening to the rustle of the jet over a field of high cirrus clouds . . .

Charley Sunby was the first pilot I had hired. He was a Russian, over fifty, and had been flying in Asia for a long time. I had heard of him for years; the story was that he had over 30,000 hours, and that meant he had been flying at least thirty years. Sunby could have been a senior pilot, or even a chief pilot, on any airline, but he had a quirk. A taciturn, slab-faced man with powerful, sloping shoulders, he wouldn't let anybody else touch his airplane.

Literally. Not even a mechanic or a crew chief. If he had a plug change, Sunby did it himself. Even on major work, like an engine replacement, he would let a crew of mechanics help, but he was there every minute, pointing and shouting. This, of course, is the mark of the bush pilot, but Sunby carried it to extremes. On any flight operation involving more than a few planes it won't work because hard-pressed mechanics sometimes have to cannibalize a plane overnight, or for a few hours, to keep other planes flying. Charley Sunby, unwilling to allow this, had nearly killed a number of mechanics and airline executives for touching *his* plane when he wasn't around.

The trait didn't bother me. The lashup I was heading into was so unsettled that I had promised Charley he could set up light-housekeeping in the plane if he wanted to. And I would furnish chintz curtains. Just so he was ready to go around the clock. The dour Russian said that was "fine," and signed his contract.

My second catch, sitting nonchalantly up ahead of me with a polished flight-boot propped out in the aisle, was not as impressive. If I had had more time to interview people, he would not have been a keeper. He was Will Michaels, Esquire, from Surrey, and he had enough time and the proper credentials, but his hair was too long. I suspect it had been too long before the Beatles were ever heard from.

Michaels had flown captain several years for BOAC on their flying boats, and had later moved up to Britannia jets. What he hadn't told me in our interview, or on his application, was that he had been fired from BOAC for heading a gold smuggling syndicate out of Dum Dum Aerodrome, in Calcutta. So I knew only two things about

28

him, in spite of his impressive reference letters from milords in London town. I knew he could fly. And I knew he was a crook.

Number Three was an ex-Navy bantam, Pete Gardella. Pete had flown off the big E and some other carriers, and looked like a good shortstop on a company team in a municipal league. Put down like that, it looks snobbish, because we can't all look like Lord Mountbatten, but still it was there. Runty Gardella had flown in the Congo evacuations as a soldier of fortune, but most of his early time had been on single-engine equipment, and that doesn't help much in the cold world outside the services. He also had a police record in San Diego and New Orleans, but most of the offenses seemed to be crimes of passion rather than premeditation. Like trying to empty packed bars while brooding.

The fourth bird in my motley aviary was Harry Liu, who was half-Chinese and half three other racial strains. Harry had been flying longer than any of them except Charley Sunby, and had been with the China Line when I worked for it. He had also been copilot for the legendary Moon Chin, when Moon flew Wendell Wilkie around Asia.

I couldn't tell how old Liu was. To my occidental eyes, he seemed no more than forty, but he had to be a lot older than that. Once, I knew, he had been on the pipe; now he swore on assorted gods that he was off it. Once he had been famed as the biggest gambler in China, often winning or losing hundreds of thousands of dollars a month at fan-tan or the card game called Three Pictures. I did know that during World War Two he had gone back to the States to help ferry some new planes and had wangled three weeks of leave.

Purpose? Wearing his impressive black and gold-leaf Chinese pilot's uniform, he had almost lived in the Douglas plant. Consulting their engineers and spending hour after hour watching the planes move along the assembly lines. When he had finished this sabbatical, Liu knew every tolerance and spar clearance in the airplane, and he put the knowledge to immediate use when he was back flying the Hump.

He and the crew chiefs with whom he stayed up all night, betting $10,000 on a card, immediately launched the largest smuggling operation the world had ever known. It was no trick at all for Liu and his mechanic friends to seal half a million dollars worth of contraband into a plane going to China. And they left India almost every hour, in waves, around the clock. Gold *tolahs,* sulfa tablets, weapons ... A Colt's pistol you could buy in Miami for $20 was worth $125 in the China stations.

After that war was over, Liu told a friend of mine that he could take three good mechanics and in two hours hide a fortune in the plane so securely that Donald Douglas himself couldn't find it in a week. Not with a team of welders. Liu undoubtedly made millions of dollars this way. Yet when he had come shuffling into my Peninsula Hotel room, Harry had looked shabby.

"Man," I asked, "why do you want a two-bit job like this? What happened to the loot?"

"No luck, pappy," he said, exposing a couple of gold teeth. So after the doctor I picked out (English) said Liu's tuberculosis was still arrested, I signed him on.

That was the crew. They were not exactly housebroken, but neither was I. I couldn't predict what the action was ahead, but I knew a lot of it would be unexpected. As the fellow said, just grab root and growl. The flying end I didn't worry about. We would be using propellered aircraft in low-level work, and the quartet I had in tow could handle that nicely.

But on the ground? There's the rub with pilots. You have to feed and house the bastards, and I had a couple involved who could turn ugly when I needed them most.

There was another thing. Solange was bothering me. I had brought her because—for the white man in Asia—a beautiful woman at his elbow is cachet. As a houri, as a bedmate, as a thing he can flatter the Orientals he deals with by shrugging off into their beds. As we say, these poised creatures of mixed blood serve as status symbols.

Upgraded whores? I suppose so. Yet when I look at the crotch and depilatory ads in *The New York Times,* I have no real desire to give the bleached and angular ladies depicted there a quick jump. And every time my attention is disrupted, while reading a good magazine story or article, by an analysis of how well my country-club lady can be protected by fabric engineering, I lose the line . . .

The jetliner rustled on toward Rangoon, and I drowsed.

Since I live by violence, I suppose it is only proper that I have nightmares. One of the worst of them concerns an American beauty, long-stemmed, a prospect of infinite delight. I have bought this erotic smasher a Lucullan repast, kept gitana fiddlers on long after closing while we sipped grand marque cognac and slipped through slow tangos and twitching African dances . . .

A body can stand only so much of this incitement, and in the nightmare I whirl away from the lady, imploring her. But all I get is a strand. I keep whirling away, tugging on this strand. It unwinds a foundation garment and some Supp-hose. It turns my light-o'-love like a top and becomes a silicone strand. Her breasts collapse, and her eyelashes come off, and she has no mouth. Her head is a peeled grape.

In this twilight land, I am so horny that I'll hunch at the tatterdemalion remnant, before it disappears, and I grope for the final satisfaction. I find it and howl with triumph, but it slips out of my hands and becomes a chasm so large I cannot cross it . . .

And at the bottom of this canyon, spading away with cruel-edged tools, are a chemist, an engineer, and Charles Revson, fretting the bones . . .

Solange shook me gently, and I sat up. Sweating. Fast plane to Burma at twilight. Below the descending plane rice paddies were turning molten gold under the slanting rays. We circled over the great Asiatic metropolis, and I saw, slightly off its center, the great inverted lotus of the Shwe Dagon Pagoda. Prome, Pegu . . . Other remembered landmarks . . . A place where a driver of mine, a nice boy named Muhammed, had been killed by sniper fire in a dark wood. While I sat beside him and fought to control the station wagon bucking out of control . . .

"Are you all right?" asked Solange, leaning near.

"Yes. I had a bad dream."

She put the back of her hand against my sweating cheek. The hand was cool, and I remembered what it was that had been bothering me about her. She was coming into focus too sharply as a nice human being, and that was something I could not afford in my business. I had bought her a new and chic wardrobe, including some good perfume.

We had done Hong Kong as well as you can do it in three days, gone dancing and dining with Pottschmidt and his friends, who were legion.

Solange had never refused a jump, and, most troublesome of all, she had exhibited a shy but insistent sense of humor. When the moguls and taipans had watched her move inside the expensive clothes, they came on strong, but she had always disengaged herself deftly.

While she was withdrawing her cool hand from my cheek, I reached for it and kissed the tapering fingertips. "You know," I said, "you look and feel and smell like a woman."

Her dark eyes were amused. "Smell better now. I am what you pay for me to be, *tuan,*" she said.

"You'll pay for that remark," I said, "when we get to the hotel."

"Pouf!" She gave me her profile, what she had described before as her "hungry Harper's Bazaar" angle, and I laughed out loud.

As we touched down on Migaladon, I noticed that the pierced-plate runway had been replaced by a more permanent one, and that another crosswind runway had been added. We went down the ramp as a group, and a Burmese major was waiting for us at the bottom of it. He was Major Andres Ferrara, who had helped me from his "Q" Movements Office in the War Department when I had been in Burma before, and he steered us through the diplomatic line. Everybody smiled, and the stamps with the maggotlike imprints banged down swiftly.

Three new Chrysler sedans, big black ones, were waiting for us before the terminal, and I thought that the general wasn't kidding. We piled into them and drove into town at high speed. There were no Gurkha guards at the edge of the airfield. The dark woods were still there, but no sniper fired at us from their gloom. The rusting British tanks that had lined the road on the outskirts of Rangoon were gone, but not the tiny zayats, roadside shrines containing withered flowers and bowls of water.

The stenches were still there, and they hit us in the face as our convoy went speeding along. In the suburbs, by the corner pumps, women in lungyis were still washing themselves without removing the circular garment. Small brown boys were still sitting on curbs, peeing at us or the universe, and I decided to tell Solange about the time they had trapped me in the Thingyan, the Water Festival, when everybody in Burma throws water on everybody else for three days.

At the Strand Hotel we were bowed in like royalty. Americans, now, after so few had been allowed in the country for a long time! As I signed for the party, I could hear the dreary string group playing for dinner, just as they had in times of British dominion. And when I had finished inscribing all the names on the registry, I looked across into the dining room.

I remembered it fondly, and it was as it had been, a vast expanse of dazzling white napery. Only half the tables were filled, because the hour was not yet fashionable. But the Sikh waiters were still there, with the starched turbans and the brightly burnished brass medallions at their waists, and the swan-shaped napkins of best white damask folded artfully into all the large wine glasses.

I told the pilots to go check their rooms. That I would wait by the desk until I heard from them. If the rooms were not satisfactory, I would have them changed and send up another boy with another key. This attention to their creature comfort was well received, and the pilots followed baggage-laden *chokras* up the winding central staircase.

When they had all called down, saying they were

pleased with their accommodations, I handed the desk clerk a $20 bill and thanked him. Asked that our luggage, together with a bottle of Bisquit cognac, a case of ginger beer, and four bottles of club soda be sent up to our suite. The clerk-wallah had been educated in local British schools, but not long enough. He envisioned an end to the great tip drouth, and nodded eagerly.

"Is there refrigeration on the floor?" I asked, and when he said "no" sadly, I said that we would require a refrigerator in the suite by tomorrow. He nodded like a metronome, and I took Solange by the elbow and went up the big stairway.

It was a big hotel, one of the best in the East. Upstairs, with a faint shock of recognition, I realized that I had been assigned the same suite. Two bedrooms and baths, both with terraces, and a fifty-foot living room. As we walked into it, I could not help but remember that it was in this suite that Solange's sister had nursed me back to health.

As I motioned the *chokras* where to take the bags I noticed that, as usual, the wind off the river was swirling the silken curtains that divided the rooms. A bearer came in with the cognac, ice, and other essentials, and Solange looked at me inquiringly as I picked up the cornucopia-shaped Swedish phone.

I held out a carefully limited thumb and forefinger at her, and was quarreling with the operator when Solange brought me the light drink. I asked the operator for the residence of General Ne Win, and she clicked off the line as if I had shot her dead. So I tried it again.

"Captain Mallory here," I said, "and I would like to talk to the residence of General Ne Win."

Click. She was gone again. Solange, at my elbow, was interested, and I gave her back the drink, said "double it," and hung the phone up. When she came back with the fortified drink, I shouted "bearer!" and a turbanned man in bare feet came into the suite noiselessly.

"Your name is?" I asked.

"William, sir."

34

"I am Captain Mallory, and I need some help. Who is the manager of this hotel now?"

"Mr. Djinguez, sir."

The same indispensable man. Once, in another incarnation, he had disposed of some corpses for me. Without a big fuss. I nodded, taking a deep drink of the cognac. "He is available?"

"Master needs him quick?"

"Yes."

"I will see." He was salaaming out when I told him to tell Mr. Djinguez that I was the same master who had run the Burmese charter airlines before, and had lived in this same suite while doing it. The bearer nodded and went on backing out through the blowing curtains.

In ten minutes Mr. Djinguez came bowing in. An impassive, hatchet-faced little Armenian. He was wearing a tuxedo, as he always had done after dark, and I told him I wanted to talk to the Burmese dictator on the phone. He was attentive, said he would see if it could be done, bowed to Solange, and left.

The phone rang, and a voice said, "This is Maung Tin, confidential secretary to General Win. You had a message for him, isn't it?"

"More than that," I said. "This is Captain Joseph Mallory, who has a contract to run the Civil Aviation services of Burma. I need to see the general as soon as possible. I arrived an hour ago, and would like some instructions."

"Yes, yes," said Maung Tin. "Will you wait a moment, please?"

I waited, and before long he came back and said, "Captain Mallory?"

"Yes."

"Ten o'clock tomorrow morning, please. The general will see you then."

"At the War Office?"

"Yes, please."

"Thank you," I said, and cradled the phone. Solange was at my elbow, holding another fortified drink, and I took it out of her hand.

35

"All right?" she asked, and I said so far.

After another drink, I realized that I had nothing else to do until the next morning, so we walked over to the Green Hotel. It was a sleazy kind of joint, but we could have supper in the rooftop cabaret and watch the floor show.

T HE ROOFTOP CABARET was as cheerfully shabby as ever, strung with gaudy lanterns. Through all the intervening years they had just kept putting bright paint over the dirt. As we followed the obsequious maitre d' through the half-gloom split by a blinding spotlight there were murmurs of outrage from the packed tables we jostled. And behind us came three waiters carrying a small table and two chairs; they buffeted against the patrons we had missed.

Finger-popping, hissing and pointing, the young maitre d' supervised the placement of our table on the edge of the stage and breathed thanks through cheap cologne when I augmented my earlier tip. While all this was going on, the young Japanese vocalist with the frightening mop of hair kept fighting his big Gibson guitar and trying to drive the song through. It was a decadent Western Ballad about a hip wolf accosting Little Red Riding Hood and making improper proposals.

He got through it, but was flatting badly at the finish, and went strutting off haughtily, his tight, sequined pants rippling with outrage. Whether he forgot the mike cord or was too mad to care, I don't know, but just as he stalked out of spotlight range he tripped and took off into the gloom. We heard him plow into tables and start cursing in flexible English, and then our double martinis arrived, and a standard juggler came on.

The martinis in the cabaret were as bad as they always had been, lukewarm with raw Hayward's gin, and I sipped mine with a certain satisfaction. So few things are constant. As the juggler went through his patter, rolling balls around his neck and up onto his head, I looked around the big room, across the smoke-filled air and the packed tables, to the raised alcoves and booths which ran across the back. They were surrounded on three sides by lacquered latticed walls, and when the show was not on, vertical bamboo curtains in front screened them completely.

Now, with the curtains opened, you could see only silhouettes in the faint glow cast by candles set in bowls of tropical flowers. It was in these booths and alcoves that Burmese officials met their mistresses and foreigners cloaked their assignations with indolent Eurasian beauties. Back at the bar by the entrance a standing throng stood watching through the dimness.

The nervous maitre d' was doubling as master of ceremonies, and after the juggler had bowed off to desultory applause, he strode into the spotlight. Trying to milk the hand, but it died on him. So he gave us all a blinding smile from badly capped teeth and announced that we were in for a treat. Absolutely. "The stars of our show!" he shrilled, "direct from America, international television and recording artists, *THE POST-NASAL DRIPS!!!*"

Four cute little Negro girls came storming out in white miniskirts, and started belting the Detroit sound around. That wasn't really the name of their act, of course, but I hadn't been listening very closely; phonetically, it was something like that. The bobbing girls wheeled and shouted in perfect unison, and I nodded at Solange, who was entranced. At that, it was good to hear an American Negro group work on the old Chicago sound their race had created, rather than have it mauled by white Merseyside guttersnipes.

The vitality of the group scored. They did three numbers and two encores and went ducking out to really beg-off applause. The spotlight snapped off with a greasy sound, and the house lights went up. It was the interval break. The waiter brought us two more double martinis, and I found that the patent was being sustained. They were fully as bad as the first ones, and as we ordered food I sipped mine with relish.

The maitre d' came back to the table, bowing as if he had sacroiliac trouble, and wanted to know if everything was all right. I said that I had been a patron of the cabaret many years ago and that its standards were unchanged. He jackknifed away beaming that jack-o'-lantern grin at us, shooting the cuffs of his frayed tuxedo coat. Glancing around the humming room, I saw that there were very few Europeans at the tables. Turbans and the little white-tufted caps; mostly Burmans, Indians, and Chinese ...

"You saw Ugette dance here, didn't you?" asked Solange. I had completely forgotten her; the question came abruptly through the stale and smoky air.

"That's right." I sipped my lukewarm martini. "And you never saw anybody do something so nearly classic, and yet dirty it up enough to make an audience like this howl."

"I know," said Solange, turning her glass on the red cloth. "She wanted to study ballet, but there was never the money."

"A shame," I said, and drained my drink. "I'll just step back to the loo for a minute, if you'll excuse me ..." She nodded, and I got up and went winding back through the tables to the aromatic toilet behind the bar. As I came back out, dodging waiters banging through the swinging doors from the kitchen, the house lights went down, the five-piece combo on the garish red bandstand hit a ragged fanfare, and the maitre d'-emcee came tripping out into the spotlight.

While he was breathing enthusiasm into his mike about the first act I stepped beyond the passageway from the kitchen doors and lighted a small cigar. To my left, along the back line of booths, the bamboo screens went rustling open. I had stepped on the match and was starting to walk

38

down through the tables when I heard a roar of laughter.

Nobody else in the world had a laugh like that. Hal Pottschmidt was in one of the shadowed back booths. His normal speaking voice was querulous, high, and sometimes even Donald Duckish when he was angry. But his laughter was the deep rumble of the Dutch patroon. I had heard it hundreds of times between, and on, Himalayan flights. I edged forward into the waiter's terrain and glanced through the cigarette-sparked gloom, down along the booths.

Potts was in the second booth. His bulky figure was leaning over a table, and he was gesturing, but I would have known him if he had not moved. The left sleeve of his gesturing arm was limned by the candlelit glow from the bowl of flowers, and the man sitting across from him was the biggest Chinese I had ever seen. And I 'don't mean just large; I mean immense. Even accounting for thirty feet of distance and the dim light, I made Potts' friend at nearly seven feet tall. He wore a plain black gown and the usual small black button cap.

They were not watching the show. The troupe of Filipino acrobats kept shouting, clapping their hands, and whirling and stomping in dirty leotards. But in the booth I was watching, Potts kept gesturing, and the huge Chinese across the table from him kept listening and nodding.

I walked to the end of the bar, where the maitre d' was drinking a brandy. The sallow young man in the frayed tuxedo shrugged when I offered to buy him a drink. Then he looked up, and said, "Captain! Certainly. I'll have a Scotch if there's some going." He had made, in two seconds, the transition from apathy to diamond-bright interest. Grinning at me like a lemur in old dress clothes.

"Do you know Captain Pottschmidt?" I asked, and he considered the smoky air until I prestidigitated a large kyat note on the bar. Yes, he knew Potts. An old China Hand, very admirable man, fine pilot. And fielded the bank note with a twitch of his hand.

"Who is the large Chinese man in the booth with him?" I asked.

"One moment." The maitre d' turned away from the bar and was gone for a couple of minutes. He came back and said the Chinese gentleman had never been in the club before. I nodded, finished my Scotch, and put the glass down on the bar.

"He is, I understand, staying in the hotel. It might be possible . . ."

"Please," I asked, and we went through the business of the vanishing kyat note again. The acrobats trailed off, sweating heavily, to a patter of hands, and my friend went charging down the aisle to introduce the Hamlet-haired Japanese pop singer. Then he came walking swiftly back, waving a finger reassuringly at me, and went to the elevator.

He came back almost immediately and whispered to me that Potts' guest was a Mr. Frederick Hang, a merchant from Lashio. He had never stayed at the hotel before, and they had no bed big enough to fit him. It took two, pushed together. I thanked him, and went down through the tables to join Solange. While the Japanese boy wrestled with the big Gibson and flaunted his impassioned cool in five languages, I tried my Chateaubriand but found it too cold and tough for human consumption.

An hour later, we were back in the Strand Hotel suite. Like consenting puppets in a romantic tale, we had showered separately and were leaning on the terrace railing, watching fitful moonlight move across the dark park. Beyond was the silver-rippled surface of the black river. Solange was barefoot and wearing a blue shorty gown with matching, ruffled pants, and I wore only a white cotton lungyi, knotted low on my hips.

We were not touching, because we had no need to. It was understood that after we had relaxed, looking out over sleeping Rangoon Town, we would go to my bed and make love. That left me free to reflect that I was going to meet The Man in ten hours, and I was hoping it would go well. I was also free to meditate, while the fitful breeze rippled my Burmese skirt, on why Potts had not called me. True, I had slammed him a little hard in Hong Kong, but we had been out in a lot of weathers together . . .

I flipped my cigar away in a sparkling arc.

"Falling star," murmured Solange, and was turning to me when a jeep with a faulty muffler came around the corner from the front of the hotel. Now, after the fact, that's all I remember about it—the random thought: jeep with a bad muffler. As Solange and I turned from the terrace into the suite, something flew up through the midnight air and clunked behind us.

A rock, I thought, turning. *Somebody from the jeep threw a rock at us, but with little arm and a bad trajectory.* Solange had been thrown off balance when I turned, but I steadied her and saw the rock rolling toward us. Eccentrically, not round. Not a rock, but an egg of ridged metal . . .

She said something, but I wasn't listening. I dived, put a whip-leg block on her, and we both caromed behind the wall of my bedroom. Then the grenade went off, blowing the terrace railing down and the room wall in on top of us.

I had her covered, was on my hands and knees over her, and so took the shock of falling masonry. Seconds ticked by while cordite smoke billowed over our dazed heads and was slowly sucked out over the ruined terrace. Her head was cut in several places; the wounds were covered with plaster dust from the falling wall, staining. I tried to struggle up, testing my legs. They were all right, but blood was flowing from my nose and dripping from my ears. Since one of them had a perforated drum already, the pain in it was severe. As I pushed up off Solange, and tried to lift her, William, the bearer, came running in on bare feet.

"Master!" he inquired. "Oh, and the mem-sahib, too! It is necessary . . ."

"That you call Mr. Djinguez, please. Ask him to get a doctor, at once."

William nodded, in fascinated horror. "This is the work of wicked people, master," he announced.

"*Jaldi, jaldi!*" I shouted, and he took off.

Solange tried to get up, but I wouldn't let her. I did get a pillow and ease it under her head, and wiped as much blood off as I could with a damp bath rag. The doctor came bustling in, a tall man wearing a European suit and a turban, and checked Solange with deft and tender hands. Then he told William to call a nurse, and gave him the telephone number. When he motioned to me, we lifted the dazed girl in a fireman's carry and took her into her bed. He gave her some kind of sedation, a hypodermic shot in the upper arm, and motioned me into the connecting bathroom.

There he went over me, standing and sitting on the toilet seat. The light in the eyes, everything. As he mopped my superficial cuts and bruises with alcohol, and bandaged two places on the face and neck, he clucked at some of my earlier scars. Especially the pale cicatrices on the left ankle. When he asked how I had gotten them, I said on a Pacific Island, fighting the Japanese, and he nodded.

Out in the sitting room he accepted a cigar and a Scotch and said that I seemed to be all right, but that he was worried about the girl. She was in shock, and perhaps concussed. He would like both of us to stay overnight in his clinic in Happy Valley, where he could keep us under close surveillance.

I said that ordinarily it would be the logical thing, but I had a very important appointment in the morning. Would it be possible for his nurse to stay with Solange? He nodded and began to scribble a note for the nurse. When it was done, I offered him another drink, but he declined. When I asked about his fee, he waved his hands irritably, said he would look in on Solange in the morning, and bowed to me on his way out.

While I was taking a French bath, I heard William escort the nurse into the suite. I put on my robe and took her the note Dr. Mukurji had left. She nodded, and went rustling into the other bedroom. I fell on my own bed and sweated through some impressive dreams. Once I was shaken awake, and the nurse made me take two tablets. They smoothed out the remaining hours until dawn.

T HE NEXT MORNING at nine thirty I stepped into a cab outside the hotel and was driven to the Burmese War Office. A warm, misty rain was blowing over Rangoon, and as the cab rolled through the busy streets I picked at loose threads on the white sharkskin suit I had ordered in Hong Kong.

The Burmese capital seemed grayer, more austere. There were more people on the streets, but far fewer foreign nationals. As we passed the curving drive of the Kokine Club I noticed that it was no longer jammed with glittering limousines. Its lawns were ragged, and the famed tennis courts were netless and needed mowing. In the days of its arrogant splendor, the club membership had been restricted to Europeans.

As we swept around the park I got a misted view of the huge Shwe Dagon Pagoda. For me, and my memory of things past, the golden spire was more evocative than the Taj, because I had seen its perfect four-hundred-foot symmetry in all moods and weathers, and inside it I had often gone barefoot to kneeling meditation before Lord Buddha.

I had a right to genuflect before this Lord. When I had been in the country before, supervising the military flight operations, I had received a late call one night: "Cancel all troop movements and ammunition shuttles; a special mission at ten hundred tomorrow." The special mission was flying a living shoot of the Great Bo Tree, under which Lord Gautama Buddha had preached his famous sermons, to the Kuthodaw Pagoda in Mandalay . . .

As I got out of the cab, before the guardhouse outside the War Office, I was hoping that the little Bo Tree shoot was flourishing in Mandalay. The stocky sentries stood at attention as I gave my name to an unsmiling officer-of-the-day. It was plain that Americans were not particularly dear to him.

The War Office looked much the same, a huge barracks-like structure, but it had been painted recently. White. The misting rain had stopped, and the long building dazzled the eyes where shafts of sunlight hit it. Vapor was rising from the trimmed emerald sward of the lawns around it, and droplets fell from the three-tiered, ten-foot-high barbed wire fence that separated the guardhouse from the grounds.

After I had stood waiting for ten minutes, with my immaculate white suit wilting and my brains frying, the duty officer barked an order, and the big gates were swung open. Flanked by two soldiers, I walked through the gateway and down the whispering gravel walk toward the entrance rotunda.

When we reached the rotunda, the soldiers flanking me came to quivering attention and saluted, and my escort was taken over by two Naval officers in white battle jackets and long white shorts. One of them asked to see my passport, in perfect English, and flipped through it briefly. Handing it back, he said, "Come with us, please."

I followed them down several echoing halls, past cubicles where other military personnel were at work, and they ushered me into a large waiting room with bare walls, also recently painted white. The room was sparsely furnished, rattan and teak furniture, and the long center table held ashtrays made of mortar-shell cartridges and a collection of ancient magazines. Just like my dentist at home, I thought, and felt immeasurably cheered.

"If you will wait here, please," murmured the officer who had examined my passport, and I thanked him and sat down. The two arched windows had no screens on them, and I could see a pleasant courtyard outside. An unkempt garden taken over by tropical growths. Green tendrils were trying to get inside the room through the open windows, and I reflected that before long they would make it. The tropical fragrances from the garden fought unsuccessfully against the raw carbolic odors of the scrubbed hall.

I had been in the room before. That time, as Managing Director of Amphibian Airways, I had been waiting to see U Thakin Nu, then Prime Minister. A very handsome little man with hairs growing out of the mole on his chin. Now, in the office off to the left, a tougher man was at work. General Ne Win, the Burmese dictator who had overthrown Thakin Nu's government and was unfriendly to the West because of what he claimed were repeated efforts by the U.S. to undermine his government.

Ne Win had finally visited Washington, and this fact had been blazoned in banner headlines by our news services. What they had not emphasized, in their deft censorship, was that the Burmese strongman had also visited Peking earlier. He was honestly trying to be neutral.

As I waited, with the drowsy, midmorning somnolence broken by bird chitterings from the garden and the chatter of electric typewriters along the corridors, I glanced at the closed door on my right. That was a fateful door; it led to a conference room that had been a Burmese shrine. In that room, in 1948, the entire upper echelon of the fledgling Burmese Government had been assassinated.

It was there that the fabled Burmese patriot, Aung San, his cabinet ministers, and his top administrative officials had been chopped down by machine-gun fire. With Aung San had died most of The Thirty Brave Comrades who had attended the Imperial Japanese War College with him and later led Burma to freedom from the British.

I was staring at the door when a neat little man came out of the left office and said, "Captain Mallory?"

"Yes."

"The general will see you now." I got up and followed him through the doorway on the left. The secretary remained outside, closing the door.

General Ne Win was standing behind a big desk covered with papers, and he nodded but did not offer to shake hands. The walls of his office were monastic white, without decoration except for a huge map of Burma behind him.

"Please sit down," he said.

He was tall for a Burmese, and was wearing pink trousers and a short-sleeved jacket without any decorations. Only the red tabs on his open collar. Ne Win had a big head and brow, and his skin was the color of mahogany. He looked tough and self-contained. For several seconds we looked each other over. I was seated in one of the uncomfortable circular teakwood chairs, and he was still standing.

He glanced briefly at the bandages on my face and neck and said that he did not know who threw the grenade into my suite but that he would find out and punish the offender.

"Thank you," I said, and his slaty eyes flickered.

"Captain Mallory," he said dryly, "it is against the law to throw a hand grenade at anyone, in Burma. If you had been killed, it would have meant only a cancellation of our contract. You are a man who courts danger. But if the culprit got away with it, he might get bold enough to throw one at me."

"Thanks, anyway," I said, and he nodded impatiently, collecting his thoughts.

And went on, with Sandhurst crispness. "You may have heard that I do not get on well with your government. That is because I distrust their policies with regard to Asia, and profoundly suspect U.S. motives. I may be in error. What is your opinion on the matter?"

"I have no opinion, General," I said evenly. "I do not operate on a policy level, and you must have known that when you requested my services."

The answer pleased him, because I got a wintry smile. When he began talking again, his voice was flat, and he had tuned me out again. He was lecturing.

"I have been obliged, for obvious reasons, to keep all your so-called 'aid' and 'technical assistance' programs out of my country. I have barred U.S. educational programs on the valid ground that they are nothing but subterfuges for spy activities. Even in regard to American tourists, which Burma would normally welcome, we maintain a rigid visa control because, for reasons I cannot fathom, your CIA seems obliged to make agents out of kindergarten teachers on their sabbaticals . . ."

There was nothing to say, so that was what I said.

"Why, then," asked the Burmese dictator, "did I request your services as Managing Director of our Civil Aviation? You were here before, and looted the treasury of a new-born country thoroughly, so the choice might seem odd."

He paused, staring out the window into the pleasant, overgrown garden.

"Although I was not in power when you were here before, I noticed that you did your job as quietly and efficiently as you could, and were careful not to offend our national sensibilities. You did not lose a single plane or pilot from enemy action, and served us well until we ran out of currencies which interested you . . ."

"Luck, General," I said.

"Understood. But given the luck, you used it." Ne Win turned toward the huge wall map of the Government of The Union of Burma behind him and rapped at it sharply with a leather baton.

"Up here, Captain, is the reason you are back in Burma!"

His voice had become agitated; he was seized with a coughing spasm. He bent over the desk and jerked its center drawer open with his left hand; groped and found some tablets and gulped them down dry. Then he straightened, mouth working, and rapped the map again.

"Seventeen years ago, when the Kuomintang was falling apart, a renegade Chinese Nationalist Division under General Pao moved out of Tengchung. Here, into our Shan States. And it is not agreeable for me to admit it, but a large portion of this hostile force is still within our borders. I cannot bomb them out. My military pilots have

47

no combat experience, and even if they had, the Chinese force has very strong antiaircraft protection.

"Until a short time ago this group was air-supplied from Formosa; its degenerate existence depended on support by U.S. Intelligence. All through the years we were fighting our own civil war, longer than in Vietnam, we kept trying to eradicate this marauding force. Your ambassadors kept telling us it did not exist. Until one day I confronted one of these ambassadors with two captured American pilots and four intelligence officers, forced down in the Shan States.

"And do you know what this ambassador told me? That the men were undoubtedly operating as independent soldiers of fortune. All the way from Formosa, military instructions seized with them. So I asked that particular fool of an ambassador not to insult our sense any longer, and the next day requested that he be recalled."

General Ne Win paused. I asked if I could smoke, and he said certainly, so I lighted up a cheroot. He surveyed me with vast inappreciation and turned back to the map.

"Lately, Captain Mallory," he continued, "this cancer within our borders had dwindled to half division strength. But, with help from somewhere, they keep their light planes flying. You will understand what that means, having been in the aviation business. They have become bandits, nothing more. This patched-up fleet of theirs is trafficking openly in opium. In addition to disrupting our communications in the Shan States, they fly raw gum opium to border towns in Thailand, and it goes straight to Bangkok. Also, they are flying low-level supply missions to the Vietcong."

The Burmese dictator flipped his baton away angrily. It bounced against the far wall and fell to the floor.

"What is it you want me to do?" I asked.

General Win leaned forward on doubled fists across the desk. "I want these Chinese out of Burma," he said heavily. "I don't want them harassed or surrounded or dealt with. I want them out."

"I understand," I said, getting up. "Your Excellency

48

has been generous in the contract with me, but I have a further request."

"Yes?"

"Direct access to you, personally, at any hour. Not to an associate or a trusted aide, but to you, personally."

"Agreed." He nodded and straightened behind the desk.

"Then, sir," I said, "if you have no further instructions, I'll get to work."

"Good, good!" He was shuffling papers on his desk.

"Your permission to leave, General?" I asked.

"Yes, of course," he said idly. "Before you go, however, I must repeat . . . a certain apprehension of my own intelligence officers. Why did you bring mademoiselle Solange LeBlanc with you?"

"For sexual congress, sir. Mine. And she will, perhaps, be useful in other ways."

The Burmese dictator nodded again, with a faint half-smile. Half amusement, half distaste. "You do tend to keep it in the family, don't you, Captain?"

Before I could answer, he sat down and fitted on a pair of dark-rimmed reading glasses. I didn't see him press any button but the obsequious secretary came into the big office as suddenly as if he had been leaning against the door.

"Good day, Captain," said the General, and I walked out. My escort of Naval officers was waiting in the hall, and they flanked me back to the entrance of the War Office building. There the two rankers took me back to the guardhouse, now through blinding sunlight. As I approached the sandbagged guardhouse and was let out through the high gates the sentries snapped to attention again, and my cab driver came sliding off his front fender.

The sun was blistering my pate, and I was reflecting that the Burmese dictator's intelligence services did pretty well. At least on amatory details.

I HAD LEFT the hotel an oddity, one of the few Americans to be allowed a work permit in Burma for several years, but when I walked back in it, I was a celebrity. Who had just had a private conference with General Ne Win. The tall Sikh durwan at the lobby entrance came to attention so sharply his beard quivered, and as I crossed the marble floor the desk clerks, the concierge, and the bellmen straightened involuntarily.

At the mail desk I accepted two cables and was turning toward the stairs when I nearly bowled Mr. Djinguez over. The little Armenian in the frock coat bowed even while he was off-balance, and came erect smartly.

"No difficulty?" he inquired.

"None, thank you," I said.

"I am so glad. You will require?"

I ripped open one of the cables with a forefinger. "Nothing I can think of, Mr. Djinguez. Ice cubes, perhaps, if we have none."

"I will check immediately," he said, and spun around on pointed, glistening shoes, snapping his fingers like castanets. Going up the winding staircase, I saw that the cable was from my mother, which was interesting because she had been dead for years. Shoving it into the pocket of my sharkskin jacket, I opened the other one. It was in the clear, from Jardine-Matheson's in Hong Kong, and stated that the aircraft parts I had requested them to transship would arrive at Mingaladon Aerodrome that afternoon on the Cathay-Pacific flight. That customs duty on all items had been given a special waiver by the Burmese Government.

The big suite was empty when I pushed through the silken curtains. I shucked off my suit and showered.

Then, wearing only a blue cotton lungyi, I went in to the bar of the big sitting room and filled a glass with ice and ginger beer. Looked into Solange's bedroom, but she was not there.

Returning to my own bedroom, I got the cable from mother out of my jacket and decoded it at the rosewood desk, keying out of the Rangoon telephone book. The message said that Frank Meyers, of Hong Kong, had fired a rocket to three top levels in the agency claiming that I not only wouldn't listen to his ideas but had attacked him brutally.

Thumbing patiently through the telephone book, I encoded an answer which said that "as per contractual agreement" no station agents were to approach me for any reason without my request; that this particular station agent was a cretin; that I had seen the man in charge and was proceeding, but that I would remove myself from Burma immediately if they sent a recall order. Otherwise, my love to mother.

Drafting this blast took twenty minutes, and when I had printed it carefully, I read it over and decided it sounded pompous as hell. That fact being established, I walked back into the sitting room and shouted, "Bearer!"

"Here, master!" William came in from the pantry on bare feet.

"Will you take this cablegram down, please. It goes direct."

He took the slip of rough yellow paper and was leaving when I realized that it must be nearly noon and that I was hungry. "Tiffin soon?" I asked, and the bearer nodded.

"Whenever master likes."

"Fine." I was a little irritated. "How about a twelve-pepper curry, as soon as you hand the cablegram in?" He nodded again. "Where's the mem-sahib?"

"There, sir." He pointed a brown finger out over the terrace, and vanished through the blowing curtains. There? I thought. Christ, that includes the Gulf of Martaban and the entire Andaman Sea.

Still, it was at least a compass point. I walked out on the terrace, looked across at the docks, and down at the small park across the street from the hotel. Solange was there. Not only there, but the center of action. Dressed in a silver sari that rippled around her limbs like water, she was haring around the park tugging at a string which arced up to a curveting, butterfly-shaped kite. The kite had iridescent wings of turquoise and green, and every time Solange stopped or turned, a host of laughing brown Burmese children ran into her.

Once she went sprawling on the grass and was almost blotted from sight by howling children. Poor butterfly came to earth in swooping banks, and landed without damage to his splendid oil-silk wings. *Pretty fair glide angle,* I thought from the fourth-floor terrace; *I'd like to see a jet do that with power off . . .*

Turning inside the suite, I found that William had the table ready and the curry was just arriving. I asked the bearer to step down to the park and ask the mem-sahib to come up, if she could find a break in her kite-flying. He smiled, the first time he had done it since we arrived, and went through the foyer to the hall. The two waiters began lifting lids from silver serving dishes, and the spicy aromas of the curry were wonderful.

I was halfway through my first plate, crumbling toasted rose petals over rice and chutney, when Solange came slipping in and went hurrying back to her bedroom. In a few minutes she came out in her tailored suit, wearing hose and high-heeled pumps, and one of the waiters seated her.

While her plate was being served, she glanced across at me anxiously. "I am a very bad secretary. But I was waiting for you to get back, and I saw the children down there in the park, but I only meant to be gone a minute . . ."

"No matter," I said. "There was only a cable to do, and I had to handle that myself. William took it down for me."

The two waiters were piling her plate high with the spiced curry, and Solange sat stiffly, like a rebuked child, staring at the hands folded in her lap.

52

"Will you eat, for God's sake?" I asked. "The food's getting cold. If you had been here, waiting every minute, all you could have done was walk downstairs with the cable."

My voice must have been strident, because the lashes on her dark eyes flickered. Across me, across the strip of cloudless blue sky beyond the terrace, and she smiled slowly.

"I'm so glad," she said, shaking out the heavy damask serviette. "The work wasn't anything, but you did miss *me*."

"Rooster's ass," I replied, forking up more of the stinging-hot curry, which would have me blowing smoke rings before dawn. But what the hell, if a man's gut can't take a joke, it should make him throw up immediately. The head does all the work, anyway.

So I shoveled it in, and across from me Solange went to work like a shipwrecked wrestler offered unlimited provender. Half an hour later we had tiny cups of Turkish coffee just below the boiling point and several dollops of Bisquit cognac. The waiters came back in, beamed to see such carnage done on the huge lunch, and bore the dishes away chattering.

I had two of the coffees, like sludge from a Volkswagen, and a placidity of the cognac. Across from me Solange groaned and fell back in her chair, both arms dangling. Among other things, she was quite a mimic. She had unbuttoned the suit jacket, but showed no sign of her Lucullan feast.

"We'll sleep now?" she asked, stretching, and I laughed. Because that is exactly what I wanted to do now, if we can allow a euphemism. Sleep with Solange, in the early afternoon.

"No, ma'am," I said. "I'm going to the airport, to receive some airfreight and supervise some modifications on our planes, and I may be there all night."

"Oh?" She had hurried so to join me that she wore no makeup at all, and looked much better for it. Her wide mouth was smeared by juices from her meal; she looked disheveled and ready for a matinee. *Bad cess to condi-*

tions. I went to my bedroom, showered again, and put on khakis and a topi.

"Shall I not bring you some food, out to the aerodrome?" she asked, and I said "no." Then she asked if I would call her before I started back to the hotel, no matter what the time, so she could have coffee, something hot for me to eat. I said "yes," I would do that.

"But what will I do, all afternoon and night?" she asked.

"Lots of sunlight left," I suggested. "Why don't you go fly a kite?"

She stuck out her tongue defiantly, but I had meant to kiss her, anyway. So I did, and went about the business of the Government of the Union of Burma.

T HERE WAS A lot of it to be done. I had cleared out a hangar belonging to the Burmese Airways, and commandeered six of its de Havilland Doves and three Dakotas. Dakota is a British term for the Douglas DC3, which has many forms. In this evacuated hangar I had almost the entire qualified mechanic force of the country making modifications to the small fleet, ripping out spars and adding extra fuel tanks.

The work in progress hadn't made me very popular with the Burmese crew chiefs. The Doves were beautiful little eleven-passenger jobs, and had been considerably gussied up with curtains and comforts for passengers on Air Burma. Now, without warning, I blew in, and everybody was working around the clock, gutting the Doves and cutting lower escape hatches in the Dakotas.

They not only didn't understand it, but started doing slipshod work in the closed hangar. I called Major Ferrara at his home, told him I wanted troops to guard the hangar at all hours and a blast delivered to the mechanics from on high. That came in an hour, and miraculously, the crew chiefs started speaking English and reading blueprints again.

For the next six days I slept mostly on the seats we had jerked out of the planes. Catching an hour or two when I could. Lurching out of torpor to check results, so that sometimes only the bright fringe of light around the closed hangar doors told me whether it was night or day. Only four times did I go back to the hotel, and each time Solange was waiting with a few drinks, and a hot meal after I had showered, shaved, and put on fresh clothes.

Charley Sunby was there almost as much as I was. He had been assigned a Dakota and he supervised the installation of new engines at a distance of two feet. When the welding torches began to cut the hatch in its belly, his broad, Slavic face was just behind the torch.

The other pilots were not idle. Among them, only Will Michaels was checked out on the Dove, and for eight hours every day he flew instruction, even on Sunby. The dawns and twilights seemed to slide together while I worked inside the closed and guarded hangar, and the other Doves kept up a continuous pattern of bumps and circuits when Mingaladon air traffic would permit.

Solange was busy, too. Getting mug shots of the pilots for I.D. cards, so that the aerodrome guards would know them. Sending cables, and acting as my courier to the U.S. Embassy in Rangoon. I had not entered it myself, and did not intend to, for fear some jerk would try to appoint himself case officer, as Meyer had done in Hong Kong.

My most important message, to proceed sealed in the diplomatic pouch to Washington, was a request for high-level photography of the field at Man Hpang, at dawn and an hour before sunset. This to be done by either U4 or drone, the pictures and evaluations to be forwarded to me. Soonest.

I also cabled another request, one I did not want to go in the diplomatic pouch. I asked for an in-depth dossier on Hal Pottschmidt and requested that a loose tail be put on him immediately. Also, after reflection, I asked for dossiers on Solange LeBlanc and all four of the pilots I had hired in Hong Kong . . .

Everything ends, and in time this crash program of aircraft modification and information-seeking did, too. I dragged back to the Strand Hotel, and sat gaunt and hollow-eyed while Solange handed me the best part of a quart of Cutty Sark, and made me eat afterward. Then I fell into bed and slept for fourteen hours.

When I awakened, it was dark. I lifted my head from the bolster, and Solange said "yes?" from the near darkness. I stretched, feeling resurrected from an Egyptian tomb, and shook my head.

"Two things," I said. "I want a gallon of hot coffee, and I want to see Harry Liu."

"All right," she said, and was gone. I got up wearily, stumbled into the bathroom, and had a cold shower. It helped. Then I knotted on a lungyi and went out on the terrace. It was a dark and starless night, and fog was wreathing off the river and drifting in low patches across the town.

The lights in the sitting room went on. I walked into it and found the bearer pouring three cups of steaming coffee with his turban askew.

"William," I said, "what hath God wrought?"

He simpered sleepily. "No man knows that, master," he answered, and I was agreeing with him when Solange came in with Harry Liu.

"Harry," I said, "good morning, or whatever. Have some coffee."

"Righto!" He had dressed hurriedly, in a European suit, and was wearing soft slippers. With his ivory skull, sunken neck, and meager figure, he looked like I felt. And his greeting aroused new resentment in me. "Righto!" indeed.

The most sickening sight I have ever seen came one night on the Hump route in the Second War to End All. I was in charge of the Dinjan Station and had all the requisite rolling equipment out when our passenger trip from Chungking rolled up and stopped. The first passen-

56

ger off was a Chinese wearing the full battle dress of the Black Watch Regiment. I have never forgotten it.

To be sure that I had a right to my bigotry, I checked with the wing commander of the RAF Squadron stationed nearby.

"Of course he's no right to that tartan," the wing commander said with near apoplexy. "He's had no military training at all, just one of the bastard sons of a Kuomintang banker, . . . It was bought for him, you see. out of money from your American Treasury, which seems to have no bottom and certainly no taste . . ."

Drinking my coffee, I surveyed Harry Liu, being briskly British although I had hauled him out of a sound sleep. Solange did her job well. I could not tell whether she sensed my distaste or what, but she fussed over him, and the steaming coffee brought him back to life.

I got up and walked around to the huge teakwood slab which was our coffee table. Spread out the strip maps of the Shan States and adjusted the standing lamps to shine on them. In a few minutes Harry stopped nattering and came around to sit beside me.

"The percolator is plugged in," said Solange from the outer shadows.

"Fine," I said. "Good night." And she was gone. "Harry," I asked, pointing at the top map, "have you ever flown over here. Right here. A town on the Salween, named Man Hpang?"

He studied the map closely. "Yes. But not as a pilot. When the Tigers were in Lashio, I was an armorer. We used to test-fly over this part of the river, and this town."

Before World War Two the Flying Tigers had once been based in Lashio, a big town in the Shan States.

"It was a dump then," Liu went on. "A few mud huts and bashas by the river. A village."

"It's more than that now," I said. "When Chiang lost, and most of his troops deserted, a full Nationalist Division under General Hang Pao came across the border into the Shan States. From Yunnan. And at least half of them are there still, with a patched-up air force."

Harry Liu got up and went out of the circle of light. To the bar, where the ruby eye shone on the coffee machine. I heard him pour a cup.

"Pappy," he said, "what you're telling me has been bazaar gossip for years. They terrorize the countryside, maybe fly a little hop around."

"Who furnishes the fuel, and the money, now that the Formosa help is gone?" I asked.

"I don't know, pappy," Liu said from the shadows. I waited for him to say something else, but he didn't.

"Okay. Can you and I take one of the Dakotas up there, before dawn, and have a look at Man Hpang without them knowing it?"

"This morning?"

"Yes."

Harry came back into the lamplight, cradling his coffee cup, and glanced down at the map.

"I guess so. Let's see . . . There's usually a lot of ground fog, and the hills slope away from the airstrip to the east." He shrugged why not.

"I'll meet you in the lobby in an hour. That should give us time to be outside Man Hpang before daylight."

"Righto." He finished his coffee, put down the cup, and went out through the darkened foyer. I sat meditating after he had gone. Call Mingaladon for weather news? No. Alert a crew chief? No. I knew that the tanks of the Dakota we would use, *Victor,* were already topped off, so I went back to my bedroom and put on my flight cap. When I walked out the door of the suite, I was wearing an issue .45 caliber on my hip, in a webbed belt, and carrying my leather flying clothes.

I WAS TURNING toward the circular staircase, reaching for the marble balustrade, when a low voice whispered,

"Master!" It was William, the bearer, beckoning to me from the back entrance to the suite. The small linen room where he slept on a quilted mat. I walked into the darkened room and half-closed the door behind me.

"What is it, William?"

The little Burmese was naked except for a skimpy dhoti around his hips, and he was terrified. "Master goes to the aerodrome?"

"Yes."

"With the Chinese captain from room three-seventy?"

"That's right. He should be waiting for me in the lobby."

"In the new station wagon, past the Shwe Dagon Pagoda and out Prome Road?"

"Christ yes, William. That's why we bought it, and Prome Road is our usual route. What's all this in aid of?"

"You must not go, sir," the little bearer said. "There are bad mens waiting to kill you on that road."

"Oh?"

"Yes, master."

I had a map of Rangoon in the thigh pocket of my flight pants; I pulled it out and clicked the beam from my flashlight on it.

"Where?" I asked, and the bearer jabbed a split-nailed forefinger into the circle of light. Unerringly, to the junction of Prome and George Roads. I remembered the intersection; it was in the suburbs, just before Prome straightened out toward the dark forest and Mingaladon Aerodrome.

I snapped the hand torch off and lighted a cheroot. "How did you find out?" I asked.

"There are many bearers in this hotel, sir."

I dragged on the twisted cigar and looked down at the skinny little man wearing only the tucked-in breech-clout. "And why should you care what happens to me, William? Or any European, for that matter?"

The little man gave me the "tik hai" sideway twitch of his head. "You will give me money, sir, to save your life. I suppose that is the biggest thing. But there is another reason. You do not remember me because I was only a boy when you were here before. A waiter's helper. All of us on the staff, even down to me, knew that you were serious and could not be bribed. That is rare."

I snapped the flashlight beam onto his face, then snapped it off again. "Your ideas are a little out of date, William, but my thanks. Here is what you must do . . . Go downstairs and have Captain Liu leave the hotel through the back entrance, catching a cab to the aerodrome on another block . . ." William must also instruct the driver of the station wagon to draw the blinds in the back seat, but he was not to leave until I ordered him to. That I would not be riding with him, but that he was to proceed to Mingaladon past the Pagoda and out Prome Road, the usual route. Did he have that straight?

"Yes, sir," said William. He was struggling into his white robe and adjusting his puggree. While he latched the polished brass buckle at his waist, I fumbled out kyats 500 from my inside pocket and gave them to him. I wanted a cab to be waiting just behind the station wagon, but I didn't want a driver for it. I would be the driver. All understood?

"Yes, master." William moved out of the dimly lighted room and down the stairway. I went back into the suite, to the closet in my bedroom. A light was shining through the bathroom from Solange's room; she must have been reading, and she called out "Joe?"

"Forgot something," I answered, and she murmured an indistinguishable reply. By then I had the oblong case open and was assembling the oiled components of the Browning Automatic Rifle. There are more advanced portable rapid-fire weapons in the world, but I had been expert on this one at Parris Island once and had used it often in the Pacific War. I knew just how much left hand was needed to keep it from riding up on full automatic.

When I had checked it out thoroughly, I loaded and inserted a full clip and tore the weapon down again, fitting its parts back into the case. All except the bipod from which it was supposed to be fired. That I left behind on the closet floor.

When I walked out of the main entrance of the Strand Hotel, I was hefting the case idly, trying to pretend it was not heavy. The driver of the station wagon was waiting. When the Sikh doorman came to attention, the driver scrambled out and gave me a flat-handed British salute.

"Good morning," I said. "Do you have a watch?"

"Yes, sir!" The driver poked his brown wrist free from its sleeve and showed me his Omega.

"Good. In twenty minutes, exactly, you will drive to Mingaladon and wait before the Air Burma hangar. Okay?"

"Hokay!" the driver said, and flashed me another jerky, palm-out salute. I got in the cab behind the station wagon and drove down side roads until I was on one of the dark lanes behind the huge Pagoda. There I stopped and assembled the BAR again, being sure it was locked together tightly. Then I placed it on the front seat and started the decrepit cab again.

I had to circle the juncture of Prome and George Roads twice before I spotted the ambush car. The intersection had a circular fountain in its center; all turns around it meant a slowdown. In addition, George Road was split by a central island, a small parkway, and I had to creep through two shadowed bazaars to approach it from the east.

The ambush car was a Dodge sedan, dark green, several years old, parked on the east side of George Road, nearest the circle. Any car going north out of Rangoon on Prome Road had to swing around the fountain while losing speed. There was a car parked twenty feet behind the Dodge, and then a long empty space. I eased my cab back of the other car, cut the lights and ignition, and waited.

My line of vision was blocked by the empty car, and I could not tell how many people were in the Dodge. And the street was so deserted that I did not want to get out because the occupants of the ambush car might spot me in their rearview mirror. The minutes ticked by interminably as I sat with my hand resting on the oiled stock of the automatic rifle. Just as I was reflecting that the station wagon driver must have a very slow Omega, I saw the new machine come roaring around the circle.

The driver had been going too fast coming into the intersection, and the hood of the International was bowing as he stomped the brakes. Tires wailed, and when he was broadside to the waiting Dodge, two light machine guns opened up.

He never did get straightened out, under that withering barrage. There was an overhead light on a pole protruding from the fountain, and I saw slugs ripping into the station wagon. Glass shattered and fell out of the right windows and windshield, and when the driver's head snapped forward, his foot must have jammed the accelerator. The station wagon slewed around, motor roaring insanely, and tried to climb over the rim of the fountain.

By this time, I was out of the cab and walking toward the intersection. With the BAR cradled on my hip. Skeins of smoke drifted from the windows of the parked Dodge, and I could see the snouts of machine guns being drawn back into the car. When I was even with the hood of the parked car ahead, I saw that there were two men in the front seat of the Dodge. As its motor started I tripped the Browning.

Slugs from my hip-held weapon went chinking into the Dodge, and I angled further into the middle of the street, still firing. The driver got the car in gear, and as it started moving I hosed him like a garden plant. He flopped, falling back, and the Dodge went jerking away at low speed. The other assassin scrambled out of the front seat and fired across the top of the car at me. Missed, and started running away, across the intersection.

I flipped the Browning onto semiautomatic and knelt, squeezing off two at a time. The big weapon was burning hell out of my hands, but I kept tracking him and, after an override shot, caught him. He stumbled and went jackknifing past the wrecked station wagon into the pool of water under the fountain. He wasn't going to get up again, either, because I had heard the slugs chop into him.

Standing there, with the copper-salt solution flooding my mouth, I realized that the BAR was not cooling off very fast. I dropped it and walked forward. When I opened the left front door of the Dodge, the driver slumped out with his left heel hung inside. He was a thuggish-looking fellow, with blood still jetting from his neck and jaw wounds; blood was staining his European-type clothes. I had never seen him before. After rifling his pockets swiftly and transferring their contents to the pockets of my flying jacket, I walked across the intersection to the wrecked station wagon.

The driver had no face left, to speak of, and I lowered him gently. There were hundreds of bullet holes in the station wagon. Walking beyond it, I found the man who had tried to run away. He was slumped across the fountain rim with his head in the water. I hauled him up by the hair.

It was my business associate, Will Michaels. The English pilot who had eaten dinner with me many times, and had conned me out of a $1,000 advance. He had not drowned; he had been sawed in two by the BAR before he slumped into the pool, and he would never need any more glowing testimonials from his London milord friends. Michaels had been a posturing cheap-john all his life, and at the end, an inept assassin.

I had no time to eulogize him. The intersection was jamming up with curious pedestrians, and cars were circling around the intersection slowly. I went back to retrieve my BAR from the middle of George Road, then got back in the taxi and drove away. Past the curious mob, down Prome Road to the airport.

There, from the empty office of the flight operations manager, I called the unlisted home phone of General Ne Win. He had to be asleep at that odd hour before dawn, but his voice was clear.

"This is Joseph Mallory, General," I said. "I have just killed two men at the juncture of Prome and George Roads. They tried to ambush me, but I sent a decoy car ahead and after they fired on it, I killed them both. One of them was a pilot in my employ named Will Michaels, an Englishman. The other one I didn't know."

"I see," said the Burmese dictator. "What do you wish me to do?"

"Nothing at all, sir. I just wanted to report."

"You have not been arrested?"

"No, General. In a few minutes I will be taking off for Man Hpang, for a look at the rebel installation."

"I see," said General Win. "Thank you for calling." And he hung up.

I walked across the dark airport toward the Air Burma hangar, thinking that when they handed out the big cool, General Ne Win got his share.

The air was cool, too, as I walked toward the lighted hangar, and I began to sing an old song . . .

"What you gonna do when the creek goes dry, baby? What you gonna do?" And then the refrain: "Why we gonna sit on the bank and watch the crawdads die, baby . . ."

Honey!

THE DAKOTA we were using on our recco flight to Man Hpang was out on the apron. By the shaded light from the hangar I could tell it had been preflighted; there were damp circles on the concrete where its sumps had been bled, and gasoline dripped from the engine nacelles. While Liu and the two Burmese crewmen threw their cases aboard and scrambled up the small metal ramp, I began my exterior check.

As my flashlight beam probed at the tires, into the wheel wells, around the tail wheel, and over the control surfaces I wondered how many hundreds of thousands of hours the airframe had on it. The crew chief held the ladder steady as I went up and out on the wings, checking fuel and oil. The tanks had been topped off, and the oil level was right.

After boarding, I pulled the small ramp inside, threw the latches on the door, and went up to the cockpit. From the captain's seat I cut the cabin lights, looked back at the radio operator and flight mechanic, and then at Liu, diminutive and busy beside me in the copilot's seat.

"All right in here, Harry?" I asked, and when he nodded, I cracked my side window. Hit the starter switches and ran the engines up, checking the magneto drop and the propeller pitch. One magneto was a little rough, but we didn't have anything high to get over, so I reached back for the hand mike.

"Mingaladon Tower," I said briskly, "this is Riffraff One, requesting taxi and takeoff instructions."

I took my thumb off the mike button and waited, but nothing happened. No voice answered. The darkened airport was silent while Liu and I, and the two Burmese crewmen, waited, our only illumination the pale violet light on the instrument panel.

I called the tower again, and waited again. After the third call, Harry Liu started unbuckling his belt. "Shall I go in the hangar and call him on the phone?" he asked.

"No. The bastard's asleep. He wouldn't hear the phone, either. Clear your area over there. Anything moving on the field or above?"

Liu cracked his window all the way and craned his head around outside. When he shook his head, I eased up the throttle knobs and released the brakes. The plane went rolling out, its landing lights blinding bright as I taxied swiftly to the runway and then swung around very close to the main gate of the terminal building. When our tail was pointing straight into the lobby, I tromped the brakes on and fed the engines more throttle until the whole plane was quivering.

The prop blast went pouring into the lobby, washing chairs and tables from the terrace before it. In the mirror I could see newspapers flying around and more furniture shifting. A startled guard came rushing toward the lobby door, waving both arms wildly, so I applied a little more

65

throttle and blew him off his feet. Other airport employees rushed into the prop blast, covered their faces involuntarily, and were whirled around.

Slowly I came down on the throttle knobs until the props were only idling, and reached for the mike again. "Mingaladon Tower," I said, "this is Riffraff One, requesting taxi and takeoff instructions. Do you read me?"

The sleepy, outraged voice of the tower operator, who was roughly a hundred feet above us and forty feet behind, said, "You must be mad, Riffraff One! You have created a bad situation here and must shut off your motors. Your request for takeoff clearance is denied."

I shook my head at Harry Liu, who was grinning with all his gold teeth. The indignant voice was that of a tan lemur with a British accent.

"Mingaladon Tower," I said into the mike, "this is Captain Joseph Mallory. In case the news hasn't reached you, I am the Director of Civil Aviation in Burma. Please give us a clearance. And if you go to sleep again on duty, you are going to get fired."

I clicked off, and we waited a few seconds. Then the tower wave hummed back on, and it became obvious that we had a real patriot up there.

"I find no flight plan for Riffraff One," said the voice, but it was awake now. "No one can depart without a flight plan."

Click. "Tower," I said, "my flight plan is filed in the War Office, because it was related to Burmese national security until you started discussing it on the air, after your nap. If you wish to check, do it later, with Major Ferrara in the Office of Q Movements. Right now, hold any incoming aircraft until I get off."

Then I hung the mike up and poured the coal to her. We taxied out at high speed, turned down the main runway, and Liu picked up the gear when I asked him to. As we lifted, gray dawn was smudging the east, and I set a compass heading for Man Hpang, in the Shan States.

I LEVELLED off at 8,000 feet because there was no turbulence there and set the autopilot. The sky was cerulean clean, and the only cloud masses far above us. To the east the sun had cleared the horizon but was still obscured by a low range of mountains, and we passed over irregular rice paddies gleaming like flawed turquoises, and silver threads of waterways.

After I had checked the Lashio beacon, I leaned out into the aisle and pointed back at the big breakfast carton the Strand Hotel had prepared. It held four boxes of sandwiches and two big thermos containers of coffee. We all turned to. The coffee was still scalding hot, and the sandwiches exotic, as befitted my status as star boarder in the hotel.

When I had finished my sandwiches, I pointed to the throttles to indicate to Liu that, autopilot or not, it was his plane, and eased out of the driver's seat. Went back through the stripped cabin to the can and urinated. Leaning with my right hand against the cold, faintly vibrating wall of the small metal enclosure . . . My output, I was heartened to see, was pure amber.

When I was back forward, with a cheroot lighted and one flight boot resting on the pedestal, I asked Harry Liu to tell me what else he knew about Man Hpang. For one thing, he said, it was about a half mile off the east bank of the Salween River, because the river often flooded there. The town itself had been little more than a village when he had seen it from the air, and he had never landed there.

The terrain surrounding the town, he went on, had many cutbanks of red earth, and the airstrip was two miles east of the town. Originally it had been only a narrow, single runway over a sizeable plateau, but since the renegade division had been using it so long, they must have put in either perforated plate runways, or had it paved.

I nodded, and the small Chinese pilot thumbed his flat nose with a hint of a smile.

"So?" I asked.

"I was just thinking," Liu said, "that if you had flown to Man Hpang two years ago, you could have landed and been among friends. American intelligence officers would have met you."

"Yeah. But then there would have been no need for me to be here. They got in trouble because of that and had to call in the head sonovabitch."

"That's you?" he asked.

"Harry, that's me. Now about General Pao."

The little Chinese was silent for a moment, staring out of his window at the brightening day. The sun had burst up over the mountains to our right and was arrowing gold across the green valleys.

"You remember General Lung, the Yunnan warlord?" he asked, and I nodded. Lung was a squat, cow-eyed tyrant who had milked the U.S. Treasury for nearly as many millions as Chiang's relatives and favorites. The Kuomintang Government in Chungking had never really had any armies. Their soldiers in the field had come from conscripts off the muster rolls of individual warlords, and most of them, like Lung, had charged the central government for something like 70% phantom ranks . . .

"Well," said Harry Liu, "this General Pao got to be a general like so many others. He is a bastard son of General Lung. When Mao began rolling down to take all of South China, Pao led the defection. He took his Twenty-Seventh Division across the border into the Shan States at the same time that millions of other Kuomintang troops were deserting."

"If things were that bad, why did they follow him?"

"Why do men do anything? For money. Pao was friendly with the U.S. intelligence people. They told him, get over the border and we'll make you a third force. To come in at the right time and retake China."

"Good Christ!" I said involuntarily.

"No," said Harry Liu, "he was never involved. When the whole thing was down the drain, and Chancre Jack pushed back onto Formosa, the supply flights started. The Twenty-Seventh Division was not only kept activated, but was encouraged to make raids across the border into Yunnan. Not very far, though. Mostly they just set up as bandits in the Shan States, and the Rangoon Government couldn't stop them."

I nodded. He hadn't added much to my knowledge of the renegade division, except that the fact of General Pao's bastardy had not been in the dossiers supplied to me. As the plane thundered on, I thought that if Pao had inherited from General Lung, "The Tiger of Yunnan," he should have been able to finance the runway 27th Division himself. Lung had made more than enough for that from supplying nonexistent soldiers to our side.

When I asked the radio operator to check our position against the Lashio beacon again, he went to work furiously and reported that we were directly on course. Since I trust Burmese radio operators like I do used car salesmen, I did the same thing myself and found he was right. Harry Liu was busy with his maps, and reported that we had better change course to the east so that we could skirt Man Hpang with the sun behind us. And that we ought to gain some altitude.

I took the plane off automatic pilot and steadied it. Looked at the little Chinese. He said he had it, so I took my hands off the yoke and said "all yours."

We flew east into the sun, and the plateau below us changed to wooded foothills and then to mountains. I was leaning back, watching the altimeter, and when it got to 13,500, I asked Liu if we ought to switch to oxygen. He was hand-flying the plane carefully.

"We've got demand-type masks," he said, "and who cares if these little Burmese cats conk out. There are plenty more like them in Rangoon."

He was referring to our crewmen. There were no

oxygen fittings or masks in their compartment because the Dakota had never flown over 12,000 feet on its passenger runs.

I leaned out and down, and looked back at them, but they didn't seem to be turning blue.

"Don't worry about them," said Liu. He was sitting straight, and overcontrolling. Even in the smooth air, the plane was beginning to fishtail, but since it is one of the unwritten laws of the cockpit that you don't take the controls away from a copilot, especially one who ordinarily flies captain, I waited and pretended not to watch him.

"We'll let down in a few minutes," he announced, as though he were privy to my thought. I nodded, leaned back, and was lighting another cigar when I saw the knuckles of his left hand whiten as they gripped the yoke. What I wasn't watching was his other hand, so I had only a blurred glimpse as he half-stood and slugged me over the head with a wrench.

W HEN I REGAINED consciousness, I was sprawled on the grass under the parked Dakota. There was a knot behind my right ear, where Harry Liu had clouted me, and I sat up testing the lump gingerly with my fingertips. My head felt like a gong-slamming tournament was being held inside it, and when I sat up groggily, I looked straight into the face of an unsmiling Chinese soldier.

He was holding a carbine ready, and he smelled like a gut wagon. Turning my head slowly, I saw that the plane was ringed by other soldiers, all armed and all hoping I would cough, or blow my nose, do something suspicious so that they could shoot me. I was giving them a break by calling them soldiers, because there wasn't a complete uniform among them.

The one squatting in my face, emitting waves of old fish-head sauce, wore faded blue quilted pants of the kind Nationalist Chinese troops had worn, but his upper body was bare, and he had new tennis shoes on his sockless feet. I glanced at him again, and he stared back with implacable hatred in his dark eyes.

The Dakota was parked just off the runway intersection at Man Hpang, and I noticed that the main runway, long enough to take jets, was perforated plate. The crosswind strip was hard red clay but would probably be useable, even in the monsoon season, for small craft. The terminal was an unsided bamboo basha with a thatched roof, and back of it I could see several rows of hangars with corrugated roofs. Behind them, a long line of storage godowns.

Still testing the knob on my head, I counted twenty-seven planes parked on the asphalted strips before the hangars. Eleven of them were incredibly ancient DC3s, of the C51 and C47 vintage, and the rest were a mixed and rusty bag. A Hudson, three Beechcraft, two Lodestars, and the rest single-engine Cubs and observation-type lightplanes.

Only one, a trim new Cessna Skynight, looked really serviceable, and I guessed that it was General Pao's personal chariot. Back of the entire encampment a road went winding over the red flats to a grove of eucalyptus trees. At its edge was a straggle of huts raised several feet off the ground, and I concluded that that must be the way to Man Hpang. I could not see either the village or the Salween River.

The antiaircraft defenses General Win had commented on so bitterly were there, too, in batteries of three. Ringing the entire field in four tiers behind red earth ramparts. Strafing planes would have little luck against them. I couldn't make out the type of gun, but was sure they would be effective up to thirty, perhaps forty, thousand feet. And the skimpy Burmese bomber fleet would be lucky to hit Burma at that altitude. I also counted six helicopters parked near the antiaircraft emplacements, and wondered why they were positioned like that.

To the east, on the other side of the field, a low range of mountains sloped away, their flanks heavily timbered. To the north the valley fell to marshland, rank with head-high elephant grass, broken by bamboo groves. South was a blank; the land beyond the main runway rose gradually until it was only a shrubbed swale.

Moving slowly, I took a twisted cheroot from the pocket of my bush jacket and offered it to the guard squatting only two feet away. He did not take or reject it, just stayed back on his heels, so I put the cigar in my mouth and was lighting it when he smashed me in the face with the butt of his carbine.

I assumed from this that he did not want me to smoke. In any case, I couldn't have because the cheroot had been powdered almost to snuff. My nose was bleeding, and as I came up off my elbows I probed with my tongue and found a loose tooth. Wiping my nose with the backs of my hands, I waited with my jolly Chinese guards. I had a handkerchief in my hip pocket which might have stanched the flow of blood, but I wasn't about to reach for it.

The air was warm but not uncomfortable, because we were at five thousand feet. After a few minutes the nasal flow slowed, and I was about to congratulate myself on that when I realized it was not my marvelous recovery powers at all. It was just that the nose had swollen to the size of a breakfast bun and inhibited the hemorrhage.

My belly was something else. It was rolling with a bitter bile, and I had to clamp my mouth to keep it from coming up. That sickness was not from any injury, except to my pride. Joe Gall, the high-priced contract enforcer, had been sandbagged by Harry Liu, a scrawny Chinese who weighed 98 pounds fully dressed.

I had violated the first rule of my trade. *Never, never, let anyone get the jump on you. In bed, on the can, or in a dentist's chair, everyone was a potential enemy* . . .

After another half hour a jeep came snarling around the terminal basha and stopped beside the Dakota. Harry Liu was in front beside the driver, and two more soldiers sat in back. As Liu stepped out and began barking orders in

Chinese I noticed that the newly arrived soldiers were in full uniform, long khaki shorts and shirts, and they wore polished jump boots.

My original guards dragged me out from under the Dakota, and I straightened up. Liu glanced at my bulbous nose and blood-stained jacket but did not comment.

"Harry," I said, "I underestimated you."

The scrawny little Chinese registered surprise. "Why, Captain? You knew me, and made a bid. Somebody else made a higher one. Please get in the jeep."

I got in the jeep beside the driver. He had not moved, and neither had the two soldiers in back. I had time to notice that they both held Belgian 7.62 F.N. rifles, which are very wicked weapons. They don't have to be very wicked at a distance of no inches, however, which was the range used by the soldier sitting behind me. The jeep snarled back toward the military encampment, and I felt the muzzle pressing against the back of my skull and thought that these piggies were a long way from the market, but reaching it somehow.

We drove around the back of the terminal and down along the flight line, past the dilapidated aircraft, and stopped before a thatched shed at the far north end. I was hustled out and dumped on a straw mat in the center of the unsided structure. My ankles and wrists were locked into iron shackles, which were connected by chains to the four huge teakwood corner posts of the shed. When they were satisfied that I was secure, the three soldiers got in the jeep and drove away again. The inside part of the fetters was worn smooth; they had seen a lot of use.

I was not too uncomfortable because I had approximately a foot of play in the chains from each direction, so I just lay on my back and considered the rewards of stupidity. Mine. But something else was bothering me, and I half-turned, clanking, to stare down the flight line.

From the sun's angle over the shed, it must have been about one in the afternoon, and I had lain under the plane for at least an hour. But nobody was working anywhere on the airport. No mechanics, no activity visible inside the terminal. I didn't understand how you could run an air force that way, even a degenerate one, but then I realized, what the hell. It ain't *my* air force, and went to sleep.

I was awakened in the late afternoon by some people who were rudely undressing me. That was a drag, because they had to unlock my rusty fetters and yank me around for quite a while. Even the shorts went. I was rechained and left naked on the mat, trying to stare around my nose, which had now assumed the proportions of a swollen cucumber.

There isn't much to do in Man Hpang at night, especially when you are sprawled naked and manacled in an open shed. I was visited by several insects, some flying, some crawling, but no mosquitoes turned up. Lights began going on in the hangars, and by turning to the limit of my chains, I could see crews of mechanics coming out, stringing work lights with them. More lights went on in the terminal, and someone cranked up the Dakota and taxied it across the field and onto the apron.

The bile had settled, and my stomach began to contract with hunger. Just as I was considering the possible nutritive value of the woven mat beneath me, the jeep came back and I was unshackled and driven down the line to another basha. The driver escorted me inside, the two boys with the Belgian rifles following us.

The place was neat and clean, filled with rattan furniture, and the jeep driver opened a door and pointed at a shower.

"You will clean yourself, please," he said in faultless English. I nodded and walked under the shower. The water was tepid and must have come from a storage tank on the roof. The soap smelled of lye but could be coaxed to a lather, and when I had finished my ablutions, the jeep driver was waiting with a towel.

When I was dry, he motioned me back into the main room and pointed at my clothes. They had been washed, starched, and ironed. I put them on, under the watchful rifles, and as I combed my hair at the wall mirror I noticed a Huntley & Palmer biscuit tin on the side table. I was so famished I could have gnawed through the metal

74

container, but instead walked back to the jeep, as directed.

The dead airport had come to life. All the hangars blazed with lights, and people were working inside the terminal building as we drove past it. The godowns were lighted, and I could see coolies, or at least non-Chinese soldiers, trucking wooden crates and bags of rice around. When we had passed the godowns, the jeep went humming between rows of weathered barracks filled with light, noise, and blaring radio music. Shirtless Chinese soldiers were wandering around, sitting on the broad steps, and a lot of them were holding Kachin women. They seemed to be very unruly barracks.

We drove out of the encampment for several miles, and stopped just inside the eucalyptus grove I had noticed earlier. Before a huge, carved gateway. The driver ordered me out, and the three soldiers flanked me as we walked under the gateway and into a formal English garden, its luxuriant beds and topiary rows faintly illuminated by the blaze of lights from a bungalow.

Four Chinese soldiers in immaculate uniforms guarded the door beyond the wide veranda, and when the jeep driver growled something, they lowered their rifles and let us pass. We walked over polished hardwood floors down the long foyer, past several sitting rooms, all blazing with light, and entered a formal dining hall, where the lights were dim.

The room was tremendous; its walls were paneled with rosewood, set with smaller panels of figured scarlet silk. Four huge chandeliers put faint radiance across the tables and high-piled carpets. The lower-level table was lacquered blood-red and covered with gold-leafed birds of prey. Beyond it, on a raised dais, with magnificent Coromandel screens behind its throne-shaped chair, was a smaller table. As if to accentuate the throne table, there was a four-foot space between it and the lower one.

Although the main table had a formal setting for twelve, the gold-embossed plates, glittering cutlery, and snowy napery, there were only two guests there. They were Maung Kin and Richard Tin, the two Burmese boys who had been my radio operator and flight mechanic. They sat facing the raised table and the empty throne chair.

The seat between the Burmese boys was vacant, and I was ushered to it. As I sat down I noticed that their clothes had also been freshly laundered and ironed. And, as in some odd ballet, I saw several other things happen.

Two Coromandel screens at the far end of the room were removed, and six musicians who had been sitting behind them began to play soft, dissonant airs. Also, as my military escort backed out of the dimly lighted and elegant room, three armed soldiers stepped up and stood like footmen behind our three chairs.

"Good evening, gentlemen," I said to the two Burmese crewmen, keeping my hands in my lap. They chorused softly in answer but did not turn to look at me.

The floor show was worth waiting for. From behind one of the screens on the dais, a man who was considerably larger than life stepped out. He was towering, nearly seven feet tall, and he must have weighed three hundred pounds. He wore a robe of bronze satin, with a richly embroidered breastplate, and a necklace of amber and jade hung around his thick neck, symbolic of mandarin rank.

He was the man I had seen talking, or listening, to Pottschmidt in the cabaret of the Green Hotel in Rangoon. *The last mandarin,* I thought involuntarily, because there weren't any more, unless they were keeping shops in Taipeh.

His broad face looked sleepy under the black silk cap, and when he took another step, bowing servants helped seat his bulk in the throne chair. Slowly he leaned forward and looked down at us, waggling one massive hand free from the sleeve of his robe.

The Chinese combo at the far end of the room shifted gears and picked up their tempo. After a few bars I realized that they were trying to approximate the melody of "Back Home In Indiana," and cold fear touched my coccyx. Our massive host blinked; his eyes opened.

76

"I am General Hang Pao," he said. "And you are Captain Joseph Gall, come to put me out of business."

The musicians were back at their muted dissonance, and the two Burmese boys flanking me were sitting with their heads down.

"That's right," I said.

"Good, good!" He lifted his right hand slightly, and servants filled the long dining room. "For the moment you are my guest, and we must dine."

The servants brought in an elaborate meal, each dish served from smoking silver salvers. The Burmese crewmen must have been as hungry as I was, because we gobbled at everything, and it was Cantonese cooking at its best. Prawns and chicken and eels and sweet-and-pungent pork, and old eggs, and blistering-hot mustard with the egg rolls. Even, finally, when we were too stuffed to enjoy it, Pekin Duck, with its flaky, crackling skin.

An hour later we were surfeited. Above us, from the dais, the general belched loudly and spat on the rug. His wide face beamed down paternally as the servants poured green cliff tea into fragile cups.

"Do you think, Captain Gall," he asked, "that you have made a good beginning?"

Blowing on my steaming, fragrant tea, I shook my head. That seemed to cheer him up.

"I cannot get the proper kind of sing-song girls in this wilderness," he said, "but I thought you might like to see a Kachin sword dance."

He lifted his right sleeve again and struck a nervous servant, who dropped a dish. Angered, General Hang Pao swept the offender completely off the dais with a whipping motion of his arm. The waiter fell to the floor before us, scrambled up, and went out backward, bowing frantically.

The music mounted to a strident beat, and eight Kachin dancers came stomping in. The prancing women wore bright red skirts and black velvet jackets festooned with silver ornaments. The men were more simply dressed, in loose black cotton pants, white blouses, and turbans. They carried shoulder-slung, square-tipped swords of saber length, the double hand-grips embossed in silver.

Their rhythm was generated by a single drummer, pounding away at a long hourglass instrument. I watched their jerkings to his beat, and half-turned my head to see that the armed footmen were still behind our chairs. Except that there was a difference now. The flaps of their hip-held holsters were open.

The star came on. He was a stocky man with Tibetan features, bare above the chest, and he was whirling shorter swords in each hand. He lunged like a cat, and the whistling swords made patterns of light around his head; he whistled them up and down, and I felt the chill along my spine again. Because I thought I was just about to be dead.

It is an unpleasant Chinese custom. You feed the enemy, give him lute song and flowery talk, and then ... I stiffened in my chair, and the immense mandarin must have seen it, because one of his hands twitched. When it did, the soldiers behind my two Burmese crewmen drew their pistols and shot the brown boys through the back of the head.

The shock of the heavy-caliber pistols going off that close deafened me. After several seconds I realized that I was still alive. On the immaculate damask tablecloth before me, I saw my dessert—and blown-out brain matter of pinkish gray. The body on my right was still jerking, shifting the table.

I lifted my gaze to the dais, and saw General Pao heave up from his throne chair like a leviathan. In that instant he became my personal Moby Dick. Another servant crept up to him with a damp towel, and he touched it languidly to the corners of his mouth. Threw it aside.

"I cannot give you the satisfaction of death, Captain Gall," he said. "You are too valuable. If one of my planes gets forced down, I can get quite an exchange agreement for you. Not from your government, not a penny to be realized there. They don't know you. Isn't it so?"

I didn't answer. The Kachin dance troupe, as if on cue, had stopped when the pistols fired and were standing irresolute on the strip of bare floor. General Pao flicked his right hand again, the drummer began beating again, and the sword dancer twirled toward me.

The soldiers who had murdered the Burmese crewmen went to work. One took my throat in a hammerlock, and the other two held my hands down. The one leaning over slashed down across the table with his right-hand blade.

And there I was. Staring at my left index finger, parted neatly from the hand. With blood flooding the damask tablecloth.

"You hear all these things about the efficiency of the FBI, and their tremendous fingerprint file," said General Pao. "If you are to be valuable as a ransom object, I'll send them real proof. They should be able to do wonders with a whole finger."

W HILE I SAT staring at the severed finger General Pao motioned, and the music stopped. When he had left the room, striding as jauntily as a homosexual archbishop, the dining hall was flooded with lights. An orderly came to pour disinfectant over my maimed hand, and when it was bandaged, I was jeeped back to my air-conditioned shed.

I was getting as comfortable as I could, lying on my back with all four limbs chained separately, when an officer came through the gloom and posted two sentries. Every hour one of them came to flash a hand torch across me, while the other stayed at a safe distance.

On the third inspection visit the soldier kept the flash on my face for several seconds, and something dropped from his other hand to the mat. When he retreated to take up his post again, I eased around and raked in what felt like a hunk of uncooked bread. It smelled a little aromatic for dough, however. When I had juggled it to my mouth and taken a bite, I realized that it was gum opium.

Before the lump was half gone, I fell into a sleep of stupefaction and was awakened at dawn by the thunderings of the rebel fleet taking off.

After all the planes were gone, I noticed that every antiaircraft gun emplacement was fully manned. They stayed that way until dark, and I began to understand why General Win's Air Force had been unable to dislodge the rebel enclave.

S EVEN OF THE lightplanes returned in the early afternoon, but it was nearly dark before the remainder of the fleet came back. Obviously these latter planes had been on the ground somewhere, not flying continuously, or they had been refueled. Sprawled under the shed, I wondered where and worked through the possibilities. Luang Prabang, in Laos ... Thanh Hoa, in North Vietnam ... Many small strips in eastern Thailand ...

Also, there was a difference in the two flight sections. The early planes had come back heavily loaded, but the later ones had been empty. I could tell that from the tires, as they taxied in and parked.

My left hand was swollen and aching, and I was hoping to God that my stomach rumblings didn't mean I was getting dysentery. I already had a long history of both amoebic and bacillary and if I got knocked down again, it would get messy, what with chains on my wrists and ankles. I had been fed twice during the day, bowls of boiled rice and stinking fish, and been given a pannikin of water each time. Between these feedings, I had nibbled slowly at the crusts left from the hunk of gum opium.

An hour after dark, as on the night before, the flight

line began to blaze with lights as the mechanics went to work. The distant hubbub of high living in the barracks began again; I could hear blaring radios and drunken laughter. At first I thought they had discontinued the shed guard, but when a group of Chinese soldiers and their Kachin bawds came to stare, jeer, and spit on me, an armed sentry left the nearest plane and shouted until my fan club stumbled away.

The relief guard came on duty about two hours later as the work lights began to wink off along the flight line. I was only guessing at the time, of course, but tried to judge its passage by the newsbreaks on the blaring radios. The new sentry squatted at the south edge of my shed; I could see him only in silhouette. His rifle was canted between his knees.

"Do not move, Captain," the squatting figure said quietly, "when I approach you."

The silhouette had spoken in mission English. I lay motionless. He put down his rifle and came toward me on his hands and knees. There were several clicks as he fumbled a key into my ankle and wrist fetters. Then, backing away again on his hands and knees the sentry regained his rifle and squatted with it.

"You can free yourself anytime, Captain," he called softly. "The irons are unlocked but still in place ..." I grunted my doubt, and he said quickly that it was true, to try one wristlock. I did, and it fell open. By levering my hand into the straw mat, I closed it again.

"You must listen to me, sir, and trust me," the sentry said urgently, "because I cannot come near you again. The duty officer watches this basha through night binoculars." He sounded frightened.

"Okay," I said. "Go on."

The sentry whispered that I was not to free myself until "first light," when Burmese Government fighter planes would strafe the runways of Man Hpang.

They would make only one pass, at low level, and return to Rangoon. This was because of the efficient antiaircraft guns surrounding the field. Did I understand that?

"Yes," I said.

When the fighters began to strafe, I was to free myself and run to a clump of white bamboos a quarter mile north of the aerodrome, in line with the main runway. Someone would be waiting for me behind the bamboos with transport . . .

This fellow had everything figured out. I lay on my back and watched brilliant stars pulsate in the night sky over Man Hpang.

"You are an angel of mercy, my friend," I said. "Who sent you?"

"Not sent, sir. Not sent at all," whispered the sentry. "I am a mechanic here, on this field, just back from a holiday in Lashio. There, a lady named Solange paid me much money to help you."

I grunted again in disbelief. "Yes? And suppose I round those bamboos and run into a firing squad of General Pao's men? How much more will you be paid?"

"Captain, please!" the silhouette pleaded. "You are talking too loud. I would never do a wicked thing like that . . ."

I lay sleepless for another hour or two. My unknown benefactor was relieved just before dawn and walked away without looking at me again. His instructions might be an invitation to bolt and get ambushed, but he had known Solange's name. On the other hand, I had a reasonably sure suspicion that my fine ivory-hued mistress was reporting on everything I did to my old comrade-in-arms, Hal Pottschmidt. The long-time China Hand I had seen in deep discourse with General Pao in the Rangoon nightclub. Pao had passed up several opportunities to kill me outright, and that made sense because I might become good ransom or trading bait.

My options were limited . . .

In a few hours dawn came rolling across the valley of Man Hpang. Heavy ground fog was patchy across the airfield, in miasmic waves, growing thicker and higher toward the swamps. I cursed the fog, because it might not burn off in time to let the fighter planes in. While I watched the sky lighten, the Chinese sentry hacked and spat and relieved himself from a crouching position. We observed each other with idle animosity.

To the southeast the fog was being shafted by the rising sun, arrowing golden light. The wind from the mountains picked up, and the white billows became illuminated. They drifted, began to break up, and in another half hour I knew it would be all right.

As the field brightened, I was given another pan of water and a bowl of chapatties. I was chewing on them methodically, without relish, when I heard the planes coming. The tempo of my jaws increased.

There is no sound quite like that of fighter planes peeling off at high altitude. First only the distant drone, and then the mounting whine as they wing down into a dive. I jammed the rest of the chapatties into my mouth and put the bowl and pan aside, listening.

Ne Win's boys may not have known how to fly against antiaircraft installations, but they at least knew how to blast their Mystère fighters down to the deck. They broke their dives over the swamps to the south and came over at less than four hundred feet, rockets and machine guns blazing. They slammed down over the Man Hpang flight line with a roar that rocked the hangars, and I don't know how many of Pao's planes they hit because I was rambling on.

My startled guard was turned, watching the fighters approach, and I slipped the worn iron fetters loose and stood up. When I bladed him across the neck from behind, he dropped like an anvil. I snatched his carbine as he fell and went running to the north on bare feet.

My back felt very vulnerable for the first few hundred yards. As I legged them off I counted my chances of being stopped by rifle fire. No shots came, so I kept haring on, trying not to flinch at stones and roots in the tough grass. Several times I had to swerve to avoid giant rhododendron bushes, but I kept pounding on and heard the Rangoon fighters' racket and firepower fill the whole valley, with the steady chugging of the antiaircraft guns being unlimbered against them.

When my feet seemed to be beaten into useless clubs, I sighted the grove of white bamboos and took off with renewed vigor. Circled the grove on the run and nearly fell over a jeep painted pastel pink, with nickeled wheels. The driver was a short, tubby Shan, his mahogany chest bare. He was pumping the accelerator nervously, and I hurdled into the seat beside him.

He put the gaudy little vehicle into gear immediately, and all four wheels spun in the sandy loam as we went plunging northward. The roar of the Rangoon fighter planes was diminishing; they had made their low-level pass and were gaining altitude, going back to Rangoon.

The road north was loose red loam, and the four-wheel drive kicked us around. Occasionally the track went to hard ruts, and we gained speed but then hit another sandy patch, and the wheels went bouncing, spinning, and the jeep fishtailed wildly.

"Who sent you?" I shouted, and the brown driver of the comic-opera jeep glanced at me briefly.

"I am Number One Driver, sir, for the Sawbwa of Kutkai," he explained as we went soaring over a bump. I had no idea who this particular dignitary might be, and clung to the windshield on our bone-crunching landing. The sawbwas in the Shan States were hereditary rulers, but not of the same ethnic stock as the Burmese. Most of them were descendents of princely rulers who had been banished by Chinese emperors centuries ago.

My time for historical reflection was limited, however, because after we had rounded the next corner, we came under heavy rifle fire. The pink jeep was taking a steady tattoo of slugs, increasing in intensity, and I knew we would never make the grove of eucalyptus trees ahead. Clutching the carbine in my right hand, I pushed up with the bandaged hand and felt a stab of pure pain.

The problem of whether or not I should bail out of the speeding jeep was solved for me. Chinese soldiers were pouring over the brow of the low hill to our left, running and firing. The jeep kept getting hit, and a slug caught

Number One Driver and knocked his turban off. I heard him try to say something, his teeth grinding together, and then his head slammed forward against the wheel. The pink jeep, unguided, ran off the sandy road into a ditch and overturned.

I struggled wildly, found that I was not pinned, and eeled out through the warm sand. The jeep was still being riddled by rifle fire, and the carbine went spinning out of my hand. I stared at it, shattered by a direct hit, and took off again. Chinese soldiers were crossing the road, still firing, as I wheeled into the dense underbrush to the north. Thorns lanced at me, and sharp fronds razored at my face and upper body, but I kept bulling along.

I RAN TWO HOURS before I could shake the sounds of pursuit. After I had broken through the grove of thorn trees beside the road, I went bolting across a wide swale of short marsh grass and had to use evasive action there because the nearest of my pursuers were still sniping at me. I ran north into a grove of high pines. The footing was spongy, and the sunless path cool, but it soon disappeared into a stretch of swamp, where I had to wade through stinking water armpit-deep.

The dead smell of bad water and decay was all around me; there were strange scuttlings as I breasted through the pools, and things in the mud slithered away under my feet. Moss-covered bamboos slanted low over the foul water, and they had slimy barbs on them. By the time I had crossed these sunless lagoons, my face was cicatrized with bloody scratches, and my chest and lower extremities were festooned with hundreds of writhing brown leeches.

After staggering onto rising ground, I flopped on my

back in the middle of a patch of blue poppies and lay panting. Jerked a few of the squirming leeches off and then gave it up. They were plumping up with my blood, but it didn't help to rip them loose. That left the pincered heads locked under the skin, where they would fester and become infected. I had no matches or salt, and those were the only things that would bring them off intact.

I was lying in sunlight, in the patch of poppies; there was no wind at all. I could smell the odd fragrance drifting off the blooming flowers, and tried to keep from scratching my cuts, where the blood was drying. Just as the flecks stopped dancing before my eyes, a lightplane came across the swamp at treetop level. I stayed still, but the pilot must have seen me because the little plane banked suddenly and headed back. I pushed off the ground wearily and ran into the shade of the nearest trees.

The racket of the low-flying plane had startled up a flock of green pigeons. They whirled away ahead of me in a flapping din, and a tiny sambar deer bolted across the dim pathway.

As I passed into another stand of pines, I could hear other small planes approaching from the south and realized that the pilot who had roused me from the blue poppies must have radioed to the Man Hpang base. So I kept bolting on, my bloody feet slipping on the damp carpet of pine needles.

Twice I stopped to drink from freshets; crouched to listen and get my breath back. The horneting engines of the lightplanes seemed to be north of me, so I stayed in the cover of the huge pines and cut back to the east. And when the high forest changed to jagged, stone-lined gorges, I went north again and was emerging into a sloping field of kunai grass when something tripped me.

At first, lying on my belly and gasping, I thought I must have stumbled over a root or a vine. My ankles were held by a vine, all right, but it was plaited. I had stumbled into a crude snare, and as I stared at it, spears began thudding into the ground around my head. I flinched automatically; when none of them hit me, I rolled over.

Eight stocky men were watching me. Their faces were Mongol-Tibetan, flat-planed and splay-nosed, and dark eyes peered at me from coarse black hair. They wore string loin-clouts, cloth coverings over their torsos, and had short swords slung around their necks in wooden scabbards.

I have all the luck, I thought dismally, staring up at my captors. *Now it's Tibetan Beatles* . . .

The men pulled their spears from the ground beside my head, and one of them said something in guttural monosyllables. I shook my head to indicate noncomprehension, and he poked me in the butt sharply with his spearpoint and indicated that I was to arise. I understood that, and got up. And when he pointed with the spear, I went that way.

I knew who they were. Wa tribesmen. Headhunters. In all the years of British domination these people had never been conquered. They were not Burmese, or Shan, Karen, Kachin, or Naga, and I suppose the secret of their survival came from the fact that they had nothing valuable the white man wanted.

They herded me along for two hours more. Through upland meadows bright with blooming rhododendron trees and across fields where scarlet Fame-of-The-Forest trees bloomed in riotous profusion. Toward the end I was so tired that I was stumbling with exhaustion. But when I was ready to fall, one of the stocky little men would apply a spearpoint, not gently, and I would somehow find more strength.

At the end of afternoon we went over a rocky escarpment so steep and flinty that it had to be negotiated on hands and knees. On the other side of it there was a strange avenue of denuded oak trees leading to a tunnel in a mountainside.

The towering oaks along the avenue were stripped of limbs and branches. Still, the trees did not look dead, and as we approached and went down between them I could see new growth twigs, pale green leaves, forking from the pruned trunks. And something else, too.

The stripped trunks had hollowed-out receptacles every

few feet, up and down their lengths, and in every one of the openings was a human head. Not skulls, but heads with the skin stretched taut across the cheekbones, and the hair glossy and long. Like little shop windows, the hollowed-out holes in the oaks displayed their wares, and I remembered something about the Wa tribesmen grinding up the bodies to fertilize their crops with the "souls" of their enemies.

At the end of this gruesome avenue a rounded tunnel not five feet high led into the mountainside. Admonished by a sharp spearpoint, I ducked into it and had gone twenty feet when my toe struck something and I fell flat. My Wa captors went through a series of epiglottal clicks, which I took to be mirth, as I struggled up again.

My eyes were focusing to the tunnel gloom, and I saw that it not only turned sharply every ten feet or so, but that the cool sand flooring was studded by irregularly placed stakes. It was one of these I had stumbled over. *Damned clever, these Was, I thought wearily. Because no enemy could come through the tunnel with much speed, and if you didn't know the protruding stakes were in the floor, they were bound to slow you down.*

After my pratfall I began counting the turns and stepping around the stakes. As we rounded the eleventh turn the tunnel began to light up, and I stepped out of it into the middle of the Wa village. It was in a hidden crevice of the mountain, with cliffs rising sheer on the east. In the little valley some thirty thatched huts stood on conical pilings several feet off the ground, and yapping dogs and rooting pigs were roaming under them.

My captors herded me down the lane between the huts to a large conical one at the far end. As we went along, dumpy Wa women and naked brown children joined the parade until we must have been a hundred-strong when we stopped before the circular house. A short ladder went up to its entrance, and while I was staring, another spearpoint suggested that I mount it.

I went up the ladder slowly, crawled through the hut entrance, and collapsed on a straw mat. All I wanted was sanctuary, respite from the pain of my wounds, the leeches, and the spearpoints in my ass. What I got was a real shocker.

A Roman Catholic priest in incredibly filthy vestments was sitting on the far side of the mat. He was drunker than $900, doggedly playing solitaire while a young, naked Wa girl leaned on his bulky shoulder and watched the fall of each card. Her dark-nippled breasts were firm and erect.

"You'd be the white chap from Man Hpang?" the priest asked casually, with an Irish brogue.

"Yes," I croaked.

"They're looking for you all over hell and gone," he said, eyeing another card myopically before slamming it down. Then he winked at me. "She doesn't understand damn-all about the game, you know, but loves to kibitz."

I rolled over on my back and lay there, aching. My priestly host surveyed me; scratched at the varicose veins on his fat, crossed legs. Spoke to the young girl in the harsh Wa tongue. She went scurrying out and down the ladder, and the disheveled priest leaned back and straightened with a bottle of wine and a silver chalice. Poured wine until the cup was brimming and sloshed it down.

"Don't know your business, my son," he said heavily, and paused to fill the sacramental chalice again. The "son" remark was rote, because he was younger than I was. A corpulent ecclesiastical wreck in soiled vestments, he went on bitterly. "Don't know what you're running from, either. Fear, pride, probably. I am runnin' from the overthrow of Mother Church. That bahstid in Rangoon has ordered all of us out of the country by the end of the year ... been here seventeen years myself, seen the Protestants shoved out. Now me, and Mother Church."

I didn't say anything, because he was awesome in his total wreckage. When I did not comment, he hiccupped sorrowfully and muttered that he might not leave at all; that he might become the Pope of the Wa Tribe ...

"Don't let the unencumbered lass lead you into wicked thoughts, lad," he added heavily. "She is only my cupbearer. Don't you remember how Martha washed Our

89

Lord's feet but was not invited to the party?" Nodding with pleasure at this scriptural parallel, he buried his nose in the silver chalice again.

The naked girl came back into the hut. She set two bowls down and lighted a paraffin lamp, which striped us with pale light. One of the bowls held some kind of warm stew, which I gulped down. The other bowl was filled with a brownish salt solution, and she removed my clothes and began to cover my body with it. Patiently removing the blood-swollen leeches.

The befuddled priest kept on dealing solitaire, and the girl, crouching over me, kept on salving my body with the salt solution and extracting the leeches. When they were all out, in a pile several inches high, she scraped them across the mat with the edges of her hands, and pushed them off the side of the hut. In the darkness below, there were rushing squeals as the pigs came to munch the blood-filled leeches.

She left again and came back with a pot smelling of herbs. Washed me carefully with the aromatic fluid, paying special attention to my groin, which became activated in spite of my fatigue. The priest in dishabille seemed not to notice these endearments; he kept dealing the cards and muttering at the results.

When the Wa belle had finished her ministrations, which included a delicate trailing of her pointed breasts over my chest, I thought that I might not live but my sexual instinct certainly would. I gave her cleft behind a fond pat and asked the priest who the Sawbwa of Kutkai was; he answered without raising his head.

"Lives two hundred miles from here," he said. "Minor pipsqueak."

"Then, I can expect no help from him?"

"None at all." He cursed, and slammed down another card.

"Look," I said urgently, sitting up. "I must get back to Rangoon, and soon, Father."

"MacManus is my name." He poured another cup of wine. "And I'm between churches."

"Will you help me?" I asked. He frowned, scratched

again at his lumpy legs, and sighed. Palmed all the cards off the mat and reshuffled the greasy deck. Carefully, deliberately, dealt out another hand of solitaire. The naked Wa girl was hanging over his shoulder again, but watching me with interest.

"Do you play poker?" MacManus asked suddenly.

"Well enough," I said. "I've won more than I've lost."

He nodded, and wiped his pug nose with the black sleeve of his cassock. "We'll play heads-up, standard stud till daybreak. The Wa hunters leave then. If you can beat me, I'll get you back to Rangoon."

I asked what the house rules were.

"Straight five-card stud," he said, brightening visibly and scooping up his spread solitaire hand. I nodded, thinking that the way he was sluicing down wine, he couldn't possibly stay alert. It was like finding a bird's nest on the ground.

"And if I lose?" I asked.

"I don't help losers," said the stoned priest. "If that happens, I'll just turn you over to the hunting party. General Hang Pao has a reward out for you. Half a million kyats. If you lose, the Wa hunters will take you to him."

"Why haven't they done it already? That must be an enormous amount of money to them."

"It is," said MacManus shortly, and tossed me the deck of greasy cards. "I told you I was between churches, but that doesn't mean I'm between gods. Shuffle and start; first jack deals."

"What do we use for markers?" I asked, and he leaned back into the shadows and came erect clutching a leather coffer. Flipping its brass catches up, he dumped the contents onto the mat between us. The spilled jewels blazed even in the dim light of the paraffin lamp: rubies and sapphires, star rubies and star sapphires, green fire from emeralds, and sparkling cabachon-cut diamonds. His broken-nailed fingers began to rake the mound of glittering gem stones into two piles.

Watching him, I tried to cradle the deck of cards in my

left hand, and got a shock. I had forgotten about the amputated finger and the filthy bandage over it. I could not control the cards, so I handed him the deck to shuffle, then took it back and cut it, and dealt with my right hand, off the mat. He caught the jack of diamonds, shuffled again, and our head-to-head stud game began.

W<small>E PLAYED IT STRAIGHT</small>, one down and four up, with no hole cards for deuces or treys and no wild cards. No joker. Father MacManus was drunk-shrewd, and knew every percentage. He never called unless he was at least as good as I was, except for a few fourth-card pressure bets, and that was Scarne, too.

Since we had announced no limit, and the first one to tap out on table stakes lost it all, each bet deserved study. Because if I made a mistake, Father MacManus might just shove everything in and have a look at my tonsils. I couldn't afford that because I wanted to get back to Rangoon. So I watched my eccentric religious friend keep belting away out of the silver chalice and I bet two pair like two pair.

The hours went by, and the glittering marker jewels flowed back and forth across the straw mat. I don't think I ever saw a man enjoy a poker game so much. He blarneyed me with ferocious humor, took every lost hand like a personal Armageddon, and often lapsed into Latin curses. I don't know any Latin profanity, but his bitches were so profound that I knew they could not be spiritual.

And all the while he kept knocking the drinks back. Sacrificial wine, native arrack, and once even drew a bottle of Cutty Sark out of the gloom behind him. After several hours of play, the Wa girl curled up behind him and went to sleep.

Once, while Father MacManus was shuffling doggedly, I asked where his mission was. Without looking up, he said that "those Chinese sods" had taken it over and wrecked it. Tried to kill him, too, but couldn't shoot straight enough . . .

"And these little baubles?" I motioned at the heaps of glittering gemstones on the mat. "Where did a priest come by them?"

"Oh . . ." The padre riffled the front end of the deck with his right thumb, then cut the deck smoothly with just the one hand. When you see a player do that, cash in, whether they call him Doc or not. "I've slaved among these poor benighted bahstids for eighteen years, you understand, Mallory. Then, a year ago Ne Win announces all of us are going to get pitched out of Burma. Visitors, we were, I think he said, who had overstayed their welcome . . ."

Shaking his shaggy head, he started dealing with the right hand, placing every card with neat dispatch. This is another sign of misspent youth, and I wondered where he had taken his religious training.

". . . so if the buggers were going to throw me out, along with Mother Church, I decided to change our ritual a little. You know? After I heard about the deadline for the old heave-ho, nobody in my mission could confess or get absolution until they ponied up with one of these jewels. And even then," he added bitterly, "I got stuck with several glass uns. What I really needed was one of those little dinguses you screw in your eye."

"A loupe?"

"That's it." He groped behind him, over the sleeping girl, and found another bottle.

I am not a religious man, but this thought was somehow horrifying. "You mean, use a loupe in the confessional booth?"

"Aye," said Father MacManus briskly. "Anybody who would try to buy life everlasting with a phony stone ought to get perdition. It's your bet."

I had a queen showing and a ten below, and bet him two rubies. He called, and on the next card hooked up

93

jacks, showing, so I folded. While he was shuffling again, I pointed out that he had a little the better of the odds. If he beat me, I got turned in to General Hang Pao, but if I won, I only got his help in getting away. That I had no assurance that he could or would help me do that. MacManus nodded and scratched at the ankles and calves broken by varicose veins.

"Worse than that, actually," he grunted. "If *I* turn you back to these Chinese sods, I get half of the reward ..."

"That's nice," I said, and studied my hole card. It was a trey, with a nine on top, so after calling two small emeralds, I caught a six and folded. For the next hour I kept getting hands like feet, and turned them over quietly. It had been obvious for some time that the drunken father had an encyclopedic memory for every card that had been exposed.

I watched his broad Irish face brood over the cards, and wondered if he might be mad. Decided not. Drunk, certainly, but on the several times when he ducked out onto the narrow porch and pissed into the darkness, he moved with control. By some strange alchemy he had cast his faith aside, cast reasonable deportment aside, but the fumes from his endless drinks did not seem to reach his head, which was badly in need of a haircut.

The gemstones ebbed and flowed across the mat, and as he raked them in, crowing with delight, or pushed them ruefully toward me, I knew he was mostly impelled by having a matching intelligence, something to pit his wits against. As I sat fighting sleep off, the latticed edges of the raised hut began to show gray light. That meant it must be later out in the valleys, because the Wa village would get the dawn light last.

I had not been drinking, but I asked him for some arrack, and he groaned and reached over the recumbent girl again. I took a big jolt from the bottle, and my lips flattened as the distilled rice liquor burned down my throat. Father MacManus watched my grimace with bleary satisfaction, and I wiped the back of my right hand across my mouth and belched a poisonous vapor.

"I'm coming for you now, Father!" I said, and his head

came up, eyes heavy-lidded. He scratched at his sweating chest through the gap where the buttons had been ripped off his vestments.

"Are you, now, Captain?" he asked.

"Bet your unfrocked ass," I said. "We'll have the sun here soon, so I plan a real auto-de-fé."

MacManus clapped his thick hands together in delight, and dealt the cards again. The first few were nothing hands, and I played them that way. Then he dealt me deuces wired, one in the hole and one showing. He had a king above. We bet three small star sapphires, and the third card to me was a trey; his was an eight. This time we bet a couple of medium-sized rubies, and I watched another three fall on me. He caught another eight.

What I had was called in the vulgar parlance "nips and shits." Two pair, the lowest. Unless you filled the hand, they were about as much good as tits on a boar hog. He was high, with the pair of eights showing.

"Your bet," I said, and the reverend groped back of him and had a jolt without looking at the bottle. But his eyes did not flicker. I had been expecting him to pass out for the last two hours, but I knew it wasn't going to happen now. He pawed idly through his heap of gems, and shoved three star rubies into the pot.

"And up," I said, shoving all the jewels I had left into the center of the mat. My motion was abrupt, and he turned his massive head to one side in consideration. *Like the slackjawed picture of Eisenhower when he heard that MacArthur had been fired.* When he hesitated, I knew he had eights tripped, three of a kind, with one buried. Against my small pair, showing.

So there we were. It was the hand we had been working toward all night.

He stared at my small pair and shook his head in doubt. Had another slosh out of the ceremonial chalice.

"What will you do" I asked, "after the deadline for your deportation is past?"

He was still studying my cards, scratching his ear. "If many pigeons like you fly by, Captain Mallory," he said,

"I may open a gambling casino. I call." And he shoved all the gemstones before him into the pot.

"Deal," I said, and he flipped me off another trey. To himself, a king. He had kings and eights showing, and my breath got short. My left hand throbbed, and my scratched and leech-sucked body ached. If he had filled up, too . . .

I flipped over my case deuce, and Father MacManus nodded. He gathered the cards. "You played it like a champion, Captain," he said tiredly, with no trace of alcoholic slur in his voice, although he had been drunk when I met him and had been drinking heavily all night. "Now you must get some sleep while I see about getting you out of here."

Half turning, he slapped the sleeping Wa girl across the buttocks, and she groaned and came up knuckling her eyes. MacManus pushed her broad nose in with a forefinger, and she laughed sleepily and nuzzled his shoulder. As he barked out directions in the Wa dialect she kept nodding.

I raked my hands once through the heaped-up gemstones and fell over backward into a dreamless sleep.

W HEN I AWAKENED, it was nearly daylight. A breeze was rustling in the tall pines surrounding the Wa compound, and I could hear pigs snuffling under the hut. I ached all over, and my body felt as if it were made of discarded junkyard parts bolted together on stripped threads.

Father MacManus, having lost his pigeon, was back playing solitaire by the soft light of the paraffin lamp.

When I coughed hoarsely, he shoved a half-filled bottle of wine at me, but my stomach rebelled.

"For God's sake, Father, how about some water?"

"Unsafe in these latitudes, lad," he said. "Just have a sip of vino and cork off again. Your friends are picking you up soon."

I rubbed his spittle off the neck of the bottle and had a sip. Lay back flat and watched the lamplight make strange images on the dim underside of the thatched roof. My friends were coming. Good for them. But who were they? The Sawbwa of Kutkai, who had gotten his gaudy pink jeep shot up and driver killed trying to rescue me? Or had this fuddled reverend gotten through some way to Rangoon?

They were interesting questions, and I went back to sleep considering them.

I was shaken awake the next time. Sitting up, I found that I was mother-naked, but Father MacManus pointed to my side, and I saw that my clothes had been cleaned. There was a pair of thonged sandals, and I slipped them on my swollen feet. The naked Wa girl smiled and handed me the garments as I pointed. She was squatting beside me, and found the dressing operation fascinating. I twitched her firm nipples and told her I was going to see that she got into the Rangoon chapter of the Junior League.

She chortled with glee, so I did it again, realizing that I must be getting well. Father MacManus was half-smiling, waiting, and as I followed him down the ladder out of the round hut he said that I had made a conquest.

Ten of the stocky Wa tribesmen were waiting in the center of the compound, leaning on their spears, and I fell in behind MacManus. We walked between the raised huts toward the dark tunnel mouth. The bulky priest was wearing high-sided sandals, and his cassock was knotted up around his waist. As I watched the backs of his sturdy legs I thought that he must have been a champion soccer player once, before he left the emerald fields of Ireland.

The Was went around the floor-embedded stakes like

careless ballet dancers. One of them in the lead was carrying a flashlight, and its beam flickered along the ranks of legs. Outside the tunnel mouth I straightened and followed the little parade north, cutting through the long avenue of stripped oaks which held the embalmed heads. We went over half a mile of rocky, rising ground and descended to a grassy plateau.

After another mile of silent marching across the plateau I was beginning to get winded, but Father MacManus was winging along like Gunga Din. A better man than I . . . The sky was overcast, with a bright edge on the eastern mountain range, and I could begin to make out the faint path the Wa hunters had been following in the dark.

We waded across a streamlet of icy cold water and moved into a towering bamboo grove. There MacManus ordered a halt, and after he had gone through some harsh comments in the Wa dialect, several of the hunters scurried around for dried foliage and brush and built a roaring fire at the edge of the grove. I didn't see any benzene or kerosene being dumped on the fire, but it flared up in coils of snapping flame and black smoke.

"How do they get it started so quickly?" I asked the priest. He was hunkered down like a baseball catcher, wiping his mouth after a generous belt from a black bottle.

"Resinous roots," he said, and I squatted beside him and refused a drink. We waited an hour in the gloom of the tall bamboo grove, watching the long field ahead brighten with sunlight. Every few minutes Father MacManus would gesture irritably, and the hunters would stoke the fire again. The morning was windless, and the column of dark smoke went wreathing straight up.

Then I heard the Dakota coming. I know they're going to the moon at thousands of miles an hour and that some operational aircraft are making it supersonic with passengers. But what I heard was better than that. It was the lumbering but perfectly syncked thunder of a DC3.

The plane came out of cloud cover at about six thousand feet on a steep glide angle toward our black plume of smoke. Went over us at about a thousand feet, with prop racket starting up small jungle life everywhere, and banked beyond the open field. Took one more pass across us at two hundred feet, and a covey of white partridge exploded out of the field and overhead.

Charley Sunby was flying that plane, and I swore I would give him a concert of massed samisens at the earliest opportunity. Just for being alive and as skillful as he was on the Douglas *rara avis*.

On the return pass he wasn't fifty feet off the deck, and two bulky bundles were kicked out of the open cargo door. They fell into the tall grass, and I led the chase to them. The bundles had six inches of foam rubber on each side. After clawing one of them open, I found it was a case of Cutty Sark Scotch, well-padded against disaster.

"The larger one is yours, I suspect, lad," said Father MacManus, and I jumped for it.

It was mine, all right, and contained a small helium tank, a folded body harness, and a plastic reel with orange nylon cord spooled onto it. After reading through the directions twice, on my knees, I began struggling into the heavily ribbed body harness. When the zippers were up and the snaps secured, I asked MacManus to come over and check me. He did, after handing a newly opened bottle of Scotch to one of the Wa hunters, with stern instructions not to spill it.

I stood up in the gear, and MacManus went through the checklist. Yes, and yes, and yes . . .

"Secure, Father?" I asked.

When he nodded, we hooked the plastic balloon to the small container of helium, and it inflated steadily to a three-foot dirigible shape. Consulting the checklist again, he attached it to the little winch and released it. The inflated balloon went up steadily, and as it unwound the orange line several small fluorescent orange pennants began to flutter free. I shut the reel off at the indicated place, and hooked the catches onto my body harness, testing them carefully.

While this frantic activity had been going on the Douglas had been flying a square pattern over the open field at about two hundred feet. When the little dirigible stopped mounting at five hundred feet, with its spaced orange pennants bright along the nylon line, the plane came over us directly again, wingtips waggling. That was the signal for pickup, so I warned Father MacManus and the interested Wa tribesmen back and waited with my legs planted.

"Thank you, Father," I said, as the Douglas turned back across the field at the altitude of the bobbing dirigible.

"A pleasure, lad," he shouted. "Drop in any time!" Clutching the precious bottle of Scotch by the neck, he looked like a priest from the waist up and a weight lifter below.

As the Douglas flew over the balloon I watched the catchfork under the plane's nose. It took in the orange nylon line below the first pennant, and I started running forward. I had taken about nine steps when the line tightened and swung me off the ground. I was airborne, swinging forward, and felt the winch in the cabin's plane start reeling me up.

In a few seconds I was up under the belly of the plane and being lifted through the open hatch. Three sets of arms pulled me inside, and one set of them belonged to Pete Gardella.

"Good show!" he said emphatically, and I couldn't have agreed with him more. Sitting on the cold metal floor of the Douglas, I pointed, and they unbuckled me. When I heaved up and went forward, Sunby grunted a welcome, his weathered hands steady on the yoke.

The copilot looked good, too, although she wasn't checked out. Solange LeBlanc was sitting in the right-hand seat, and her pale blue sari tightened as she pulled my head down. She was full of static electricity, trembling, talking too fast, and I put my hand over her generous mouth. I could feel her lips quivering under my fingers.

"Thanks a lot, Charley Brown," I said to Sunby. "It was done smoother than a duck's butt."

His troglodyte face creased in rare mirth. "You're welcome, Linus," he answered, and banked, climbing to a southwest course. "Next stop is Rangoon town . . ."

WE HAD A PARTY that night in the Strand Hotel suite. Major Ferrara brought his wife, a dimpled, laughing Burmese girl in an expensive evening gown, and Pete Gardella arrived on triple-stitched cowboy boots with a tall American blonde on his arm. She was a code clerk from the U.S. Embassy and seemed a swinging type, but I wished he hadn't brought her. Charley Sunby came late, and sat watching the rest of us with disapproval, sipping ginger beer.

It was nearly midnight before we got around to the twelve-pepper curry, and after two before Pete Gardella and his date lurched happily down the hall. Sunby had left immediately after eating dinner—I suspect because he just tuned people out when they chatted about anything but flying. Solange had been a gracious hostess, and I noticed that she took especial care not to let Mrs. Ferrara, the tiny Burmese woman, feel left out of things.

As I sprawled on the sofa sipping cognac Solange fluttered around attempting to stack all the ashtrays, dirty dishes, and partial drinks on the huge teakwood coffee table. I told her to knock it off, that the waiters would take care of it in the morning, and to have William dismiss the durwans. She steepled her hands under her nose in obedience, and whirled away through the blowing curtains.

The durwans were armed Sikh guards I had ordered posted before the elevators, stairway, and both entrances to the suite. One of them was on permanent night duty before the front entrance, and William normally took charge of the rear door, opening into the linen room where he slept. But tonight he had helped serve.

Solange came back through the blowing curtains, took

the last sip from her depleted champagne glass, and gave a light, involuntary belch. Said, "Oh my Godness!" and clapped both hands over her mouth.

"Wear it in good health," I commented, and she made a face at me. Acting the proper lady as hostess had been somewhat restricting to her natural high spirits, and now she was compensating. Went swaying languidly toward the arched doorway of her bedroom, looked back à la Dietrich over her bare shoulder, and asked with studied hauteur, "won't you be coming to bed, Captain?"

"Presently," I said, and she nodded, flirted the hem of the sari up over her tanned legs, and did a violent burlesque bump before passing out of sight. I began laughing, wondering where in the hell she had learned *that*. Then I poured another half glass of brandy and lighted a cigar, casting up accounts ...

I now knew the physical layout of Man Hpang, had met General Hang Pao, and this information had cost me only one finger. I had an ally of sorts in Father MacManus, the alcoholic priest. Sunby was as good a pilot as I had heard he was, and Gardella seemed to be solid. Solange LeBlanc had saved, or at least prolonged, my life by flying to Lashio with Major Ferrara. And with him, working through the Sawbwa of Kutkai, had spotted and bribed one of the Man Hpang mechanics on the loose in a Lashio whorehouse.

These things were all credits, ostensibly. Still I was certain that Solange was reporting on my actions to Hal Pottschmidt. This in itself didn't make her a traitor, because everything in Asia was done by reference. You did somebody a favor, and they kept you informed. Something important, damaging, or valuable *might* turn up. The life of every white man in Asia was so closely knit to personal services by natives or half-natives that such surveillance was the rule.

The left the big question hanging. Would the laughing Eurasian girl keep turning the key on me, and get me killed?

Even more disquieting in the long run was the fact that all my priority requests to the agency had been ignored.

No high-altitude photographs of Man Hpang and its environs had been sent; no dossiers had been forwarded. That meant that the people who had contracted my services were either deliberately standing mute, or that Burmese intelligence was intercepting. This latter possibility didn't seem plausible because anything that came to me in U.S. Rangoon Embassy pouch could certainly have been delivered.

If they wanted it delivered. Frank Meyers, my friend in Hong Kong, had been stationmaster there a long time and undoubtedly had many contacts in the Rangoon Embassy. The only remaining block I could see was that the director of the agency, a staunch military cretin, had just been fired, and so there was probably a no-holds-barred fight for power going on back in Washington. That happens, too, but such political infighting was not supposed to affect the safety of agents in the field . . .

I slipped off my flight boots and went down the dark passage to William's little room. It had a closed odor of sweat and chutney and betel nut, and when I murmured his name, the dark little man came off his floor mat immediately. Stood up fumbling at his dhoti in the dim light from the hallway.

"Master?"

"Do you know Captain Pottschmidt, William?"

"Very well, sir. He has stayed here many times, for many years."

"Has he been here to see the mem-sahib Solange while I was gone?"

"No, sir," said the little brown man promptly. "But he has called her a number of times on the telephone."

"Unhunh. Local calls, from here in Rangoon, or from Hong Kong?"

"Both, sir."

I peeled five hundred-kyat notes from the case in my bush-jacket pocket and handed them to him. "In future, William, you will keep a record of his calls, what time they are made and where they come from. Do you understand?"

"Yes, master."

"If more money is required, for the telephone operators or Mr. Djinguez, the manager, let me know. Also, Captain Pottschmidt was in the cabaret garden of the Green Hotel on the night the hand grenade was thrown into this suite, injuring the mem-sahib Solange and myself. I want to know when Captain Potts came to town on that visit, where he stayed that night, and when he left. For what place."

"Just so, sir," said William, and salaamed from the forehead to the mouth to the heart as I turned to go. Back in the sitting room I crossed to the couch and fitted my flight boots back on. Went clumping in to Solange's bedroom. She was curled up, with a shorty nightgown revealing most of her ivory charms, peering mischievously over a copy of *Mad* magazine, and watched as I sat on the edge of her bed and undressed.

THREE DAYS LATER, just before twilight, Pete Gardella and I parachuted back into the meadow north of the Wa village. We jumped from six hundred feet, using chutes of black nylon, and our jump suits were of the same somber material. Charley Sunby had eased us in, flying Dakota *X-Ray*, and we went out the back door with no preliminary flight pattern. After we were down, and clawing at our shroud lines to collapse the black chutes, Sunby banked sharply, and his Burmese crewmen nearly brained us when they kicked out the cargo at less than two hundred feet.

The cargo was in three important groups. First out the cargo door was the bulky bundle of small magnetic beacons; they were the reason we had come. Second out were the hoist-rescue bundles, which we would use when and if Sunby picked us up on schedule the next morning at dawn. Third, and bulkiest, were five hundred chatties of salt for the Wa tribesmen, about 800 pounds of the commodity they needed most to survive.

The salt was my thanks to the stocky little aborigines for not ignoring Father MacManus and turning me in to General Hang Pao for the huge reward.

After Gardella and I had lunged around like headless chickens, escaping the plummeting bundles of cargo, we waved for the Wa hunters to come help collect them. Father MacManus was first out of the bamboo grove; cassock knotted up around his waist, he came striding across the meadow and beamed on me and shook hands with Gardella.

"Imps of Satan, surely," he announced, "come at day's end to affright us all."

"That's right, Father," I said, "but those orange bundles are pure salt, five hundred chatties."

The Irishman stared at me, eyes still bloodshot, robes still filthy. "That will save the life of this village for a long time, Captain," he said quietly. "These people have to buy it through Indians in Lashio and they get cheated badly. You will be remembered here."

He started shouting at the Wa hunters furiously, and they rushed out through the hip-high kunai grass to collect the orange bundles. When they were stacked, I had them arrange the other rubber-cased bundles in another pile, and when I had checked them all, MacManus started assigning loads to each Wa.

"Just a minute," I said, and started searching through the salt bales. The one next to the bottom had a black "X" marked on it, and I jerked it out. "This one's not salt, Father," I said. "It's four cases of Cutty Sark. Tonight the Pope of the Was can hold High Mass."

MacManus shook his unkempt head sorrowfully. "Lad," he said, "you must not blaspheme . . ." And then the bloodshot blue eyes rolled. "On the other hand, we must be properly thankful for all our gifts . . ." And he began to tear the constricting aluminum bands off the bale with his bare hands. Gardella and I watched in amazement, because the instructions said you needed a certain kind of cutting tool, which he had.

The padre snapped those metal bindings like threads and had the bale stripped in no time. The Wa hunters were watching him impassively. When he had freed a bottle and taken a deep draught out of it, they watched him wipe his chin. The twilight was full, and when he began to roar again, they shouldered the bales, and we passed through the cathedral stillness of the tall bamboo grove and over the rocky uplands to the Wa village.

In two hours we were in the village. Because of the moonless night, Gardella had not been able to see the avenue of denuded oaks with their niche-displayed heads, and I had not felt like telling him about them. Several of the hunters along our line of march had kept flashing hand torches downward on the dim trail, so that all he had seen was the legs of the winding column.

While we were ducking through the tunnel, with Gardella's left hand on my shoulder, he snickered and said, "This wino priest is a real kick, ain't he, pappy?"

The remark echoed ahead through the tunnel, and I whirled to take him by the throat. "Kid," I said, in a natural voice—because I knew a whisper would echo worse—"any chance we have of getting back out of here alive rests with Father MacManus."

I guess I throttled him too hard, because he jerked away, gasping. The little Wa hunters behind us waited patiently, and finally we moved out again. This time Gardella did not put his hand back on my shoulder, and after a few angry strides hit a protruding stake and pitched forward on his face. I stopped without turning and waited for him to get up. He did it slowly, and followed me without further comment.

Father MacManus, Gardella, myself, and the smiling young Wa girl sat for another hour up in the big, circular house on stilts.

MacManus tried to inveigle me into another stud game, but I refused. So he sat slugging the Scotch and playing solitaire. Gardella would have liked a few words alone with the nearly naked girl, but I put the news to him like a meat axe. If he got even slightly out of line, had one drink, or made one pass, he would not go back to Rangoon with me. And if he didn't, the Was probably would eat him.

He was shook at this news, and glanced at MacManus. The padre was busy cheating at his solitaire, but he nodded without lifting his head and said the tribesmen were, indeed, cannibals.

The chance of local action in the Wa village being thus proscribed, Gardella went through a short seminar with me. I had no way of knowing exactly when the work lights went out along the Man Hpang flight line, but it had seemed to be about 10:30 or 11 o'clock. And from what I had been able to see, there had not been more than eight sentry posts along the line before the hangars. We were not concerned with antiaircraft emplacements or hard standings for helicopters.

And we did not want to damage anything. If possible, we did not want to leave any sign that we had been there at all. By the pale light of the paraffin lamp I showed Gardella one of the small magnetic beacons that we hoped to attach to the underside of every plane along the Man Hpang flight line. The beacons were about 8 inches long, 4 inches wide, ½ inch thick, and wafer light. Most of the planes in the renegade fleet were small, fixed-gear craft. The magnetic beacons would be planted directly under their bellies between the wheels.

On the few larger craft with retractible gear the choice placement was just behind the wheel well, where the gear action would not touch them. The little beacons were powered by cadmium batteries and had a transmitting life of 400 hours.

Gardella handled a few of the lightweight beacons and nodded. I showed him the pouch of ether pads, and explained that we could, of course, go at the eight sentries like commandos, killing them all, but it wouldn't help our case much. That was why we had the ether pads. If we caught the guards malingering, which most of this sad air force was doing, we could knock them out with the ether pads, effective for only an hour, and they would never report what had happened while they were goofing off.

We could plant our beacons and get away free, I said hopefully.

Pete Gardella had been around awhile. He had been a U.S. Navy pilot, and an inmate of two federal and several state lockups. He looked at me, shook his head in resignation, and said, "Sure, sure, pappy. But don't shit an old shitter. We're bound to meet some patriots."

I showed him the other kit. The long kukri knife, the shorter one, the acid pencil, and the coil of garrote leather. He didn't need any tutelage on any of them. We put on our close-fitting black nylon helmets, and I blacked his face and then mine.

When I asked Father MacManus if we could have a drink of his Scotch before we left, he poured us both a stout dollop and said that he would not like to be ahead of us. That our guides were waiting below.

Gardella tossed his drink down, licked at his lips nervously, and followed me out of the hut. We went down the ladder to meet the waiting Wa hunters. With our shoulder-slung bags of beacons and weapons we walked through the village and entered the tunnel, torch beams crisscrossing our ankles.

THE WA HUNTERS stayed behind when we got to the stand of white bamboos north of the field. They had agreed to wait there for three hours; if we returned in that time, they would guide us back. As Gardella and I struck out south, the little warriors were slumping to their haunches, lighting up twisted cheroots.

The moon was in the first quarter, scimitar gold paling over the Burmese valley. There was a high overcast, and scudding clouds kept blotting out the moonlight. Pete and I struck out for the far side of the runway, and I imagined that we would be hard to pick out of the shadows in our black jump suits.

Still, we didn't take any chances. When we were several hundred yards from the northernmost antiaircraft gun emplacement, I put two fingers on Gardella's blackened cheek, and he nodded and moved away. We both dropped to our bellies and converged on the emplacement, crawling on our hands and knees.

I waited for several minutes, motionless on the ground, off the edge of the emplacement. No sound came, so I unhooked the bags and scrambled down beside the sky-tilted gun, moonlight glinting on my kukri knife. The gun was secured and the gunners gone, probably contributing to the raucous din floating over from behind the darkened flight line.

When I gave my low, passably authentic quail whistle, Pete came wriggling down beside me. I reminded him again where the four hard standings for the helicopters were, all on this side of the field, and said it was possible that they might be guarded. This was only a precaution, because we did not intend to bug the helicopters. But we had to pass them to get to the south end of the flight line. From there we would work back up.

We found our first sentry where I had thought he would be, squatting in the shadow of the southernmost plane. Gardella and I had split again and were prone on the ground, flanking him. Waiting until a cloud cleared the sickle moon, I signaled for Pete to stay where he was. Then I went creeping under the fuselage of the plane and put a hammerlock on the drowsing guard, from behind.

He started thrashing around, kicking and trying to shout, but I was punishing his trachea hard. With my left hand I slammed the ether pad over his flattened nose and let him writhe in diminishing wildness. He smelled like Saturday night in a gut wagon, but then I'm told that the

Chinese say we stink. I agree that this is possible, but hope it is not the same smell.

When the sentry was limp, I dropped him and carefully put the ether pad back in my right thigh pocket. Then I lay on my back and centered one of the little metal beacons on the underside of the plane's fuselage. It was magnetic, all right; when it was still six or eight inches from the metal underbelly of the plane, it damned near pulled out of my hands, smacking into place. I tested it for firm attachment and could not budge it.

Rolling out from under, I motioned north, and Danny moved up beyond the next parked plane. He lay in the shadows about forty feet away while I attached another of the little beacons. Slowly, in this fashion, we worked up the flight line. We did not find another sentry until we were even with the south end of the darkened basha, which was the operations office.

I was kneeling under the Cessna Skynight, General Pao's chariot, trying to figure out where to attach the beacon, when there was a hoarse challenge in Chinese; a soldier came charging out of the basha. He was holding a carbine leveled, and I rolled away toward the field side, knowing that if the carbine started to spray, I was a dead man.

I'll never know why he didn't fire. I was in plain view, flat on the ground in bright moonlight, helpless. Perhaps he thought I was stealing gasoline or parts, but whatever the reason, he waited too long. Gardella lunged up behind him like a detached shadow and clubbed him senseless. Then dragged him back into the lightless basha. I waited for an outcry, for the sound of running feet, an alarm . . .

None came. The radios kept blaring back in the barracks, and the sounds of revelry were unabated. After I had fitted the Cessna with a beacon, I crawled into the operations basha. Gardella was squatting by the limp form, and I could smell the ether.

"You didn't kill him?" I whispered.

"Christ, no! These slopeheads have iron skulls."

I squatted on my heels and decided that it wasn't enough to knock this cat out. We had to make it a little harder for him, or he would have a wild story to tell. Motioning to Gardella to stay put, I went out of the basha and found a bucket in the hangar. It was partly filled with oil, but I emptied that out and took it back to the Skynight. Opened a wing sump and filled the bucket halfway with petrol, then turned and motioned to Gardella.

He came out of the basha backward, dragging the limp sentry by the armpits. We put him under the sump, doused him good with aviation gasoline and left him sprawled with one hand in the bucket. Then we gave him enough more ether for several hours of major surgery. My thought was that he would be shot the next morning as a thief of their precious petrol.

There were only two more sentries on the north end of the flight line, and one of them was sound asleep. We made it deeper. The other one was, of all things, taking a crap and hence extremely vulnerable to a hammerlock from the rear. I may even have given him a little extra pressure, because he had not taken the trouble to get more than ten feet from the planes he was guarding. As I fed him the knockout pad my nose was wrinkling with distaste. You get a very messy airport with people like that around.

That finished the bugging of the flight line. While Gardella stood watch outside the sideless basha where I had been chained I counted the ether pads in my thigh pocket, made sure we had left nothing behind. The count was correct, and we went fading over the swale to the north.

When we were safely screened behind the white bamboos, I put the flashlight beam on my wristwatch. The whole operation had taken two hours and thirteen minutes. The Wa warriors were still hunkered down, watching us, and when I nodded, we took off to the north. Father MacManus was playing solitaire in his conical hut and he nodded greetings.

His cupbearer, the naked girl, went somewhere and brought us back two bowls of hot stew. Gardella was ripping off his jump suit, letting his stew cool. He stretched, and looked across at me. "Now, pappy-san," he requested with mock-politeness, "would it be all right if I had a belt or two?"

I grinned into my bowl. "Yes, sir. And when we get back to Rangoon, I'm going to double your danger money. The way you took that boy with the carbine off my back was champion."

"I knocked his friggin' Asiatic brains out, didn't I?" said Gardella. And turned to the cross-legged priest. "Now, Padre, if you gave me a bottle of your Cutty Sark, I would fly you up a case next week in return."

"Lad," said MacManus, "say no more." He reached behind him as though he had plumb-bobbed the distance to the Scotch, flourished out a bottle, and handed it to Pete.

My associate ripped off the foil, jerked the cork, and let the pale fluid ripple down his throat. He was still wound tight, and he had a right to be. Father MacManus eyed him with benevolence, out of bloodshot-blue Irish eyes.

"Tell me, Captain Gardella," he asked, "do you ever have a go at cards? Like, say, a few sociable hands of poker?"

Gardella, slum-product and U.S. Navy pilot, dragged a hand over his mouth. Said, "Well, Reverend, I used to play with my sisters, at home. What kind of stakes did you have in mind?"

Father MacManus beamed, reached back unerringly for the casket, and spilled its glittering load of gemstones across the mat. Gardella put the Scotch bottle in the corner of his mouth and sucked on it. "What ho, Father!" he announced. "Just name your game and deal the dukaties . . ."

They were still at it, with the giggling Wa girl acting as bottle caddy, when I fell asleep.

The next morning, an hour after dawn, Charley Sunby brought Dakota *X-Ray* down over the meadow at treetop level. One after the other he speared the lines below the small yellow helium dirigibles, and Gardella and I were winched aboard. Kneeling beside the open hatch, we waved good-bye and thanks to the receding figures of Father MacManus and the Wa tribesmen below. Gardella had lost nearly $1,800 in cash and IOU's to the friendly neighborhood priest.

For the next eight days Sunby, Gardella, and I tracked the rebel fleet on its missions. The small automatic beacons attached to General Pao's planes were operational only when airborne, and because of that and the fact that the Man Hpang aircraft seldom flew over two or three thousand feet high, our job was not difficult. We were using the stripped-down Doves, with Burmese copilots, and could stooge along over an overcast or broken cloud formations while we kept our direction finders locked onto one of the beacons.

When the DF needle flopped, we knew that the particular plane we were homing on had landed somewhere, and then we had to dive down close enough to establish the place of landing. This was the only dangerous part of our surveillance. After five days of it, two clear patterns began to emerge.

Most of General Pao's seedy chariots were flying across Laos at low altitude and making airdrops below the 17th parallel in South Viet Nam. Principally around Dac Bla. While the main part of the rebel fleet was making this milk run, at least seven or eight planes were going straight south every day into Thailand. They landed there on dirt strips around Chiangmai, a town in the northwest.

After collating the results of our survey flights, I came to the conclusion that the principal job of the Man Hpang fleet was to provide a food kickoff service, mostly rice, for the Viet Cong. This was understandable because U.S. chemical spraying of the paddies in that area had severely curtailed the rice crops. The lesser flights to Chiangmai were, I concluded, more profitable. They made no sense unless the planes involved were an opium fleet.

Washington had not even acknowledged my previous requests, marked urgent, so I concluded that my old friend in Hong Kong had somehow boxed me off. At the end of our tenth day of tracking the renegade fleet the signals from the automatic beacons were appreciably weaker, and I decided that we had learned all we could from that source.

I couldn't wait for the Washington responses. The operation was getting talked about locally, and I had to refuse two requests for interviews from Rangoon newspapers. And our embassy helped by issuing a statement that "Captain Joseph Mallory" was a U.S. citizen, but had not checked in with them. Hence they were unable to comment on his employment as Director of Civil Aviation in Burma.

This statement appeared in the Rangoon *Mail* on a Thursday, and the next morning at three I took off in Dakota *Yoke* for Calcutta. Solange went with me.

W E LANDED AT Dum Dum Aerodrome an hour before dawn, and I told the Burmese crewmen that they could make the coffee shop one at a time but that I wanted someone to supervise the topping of the tanks and the oil measurement. At least one of them was to stand guard on the Dakota while we were gone.

Our ride into Calcutta was like going back in time to the day when I had spent my holidays in that city. When it was blacked out, and Jimmy Scoff had come surging into the British-American Club through blackout curtains and tossed $30,000 U.S., in twenty-dollar bills, into the

air over the CNAC table. And our proper British counter-
parts had sniffed over their cheap Gin-And-Its and said
"cheeky blighter!" And the jumped-up babus and failed
B.A.'s had heard the popping of our champagne corks and
liked us no better . . .

And the Japanese Mitsis had left Rangoon and hit the
Kitapore Docks right in the middle, while we counted the
crump-crumps of falling sticks of bombs from our private
room in the most exclusive whorehouse on Kariah Road.
Some of us had sought audience with courtesans who
occupied whole marble piles on that road, Tangerine and
Barbara and Madami, and the ticket was a hundred
dollars a go. And if you showed up drunk, Jack, the but-
ler gave you a raincheck . . .

Our cab, with the inevitable towering Sikh hunched in
front, roared past the Jain Temple in tinny thunder. I
remembered the tremendous sacred carp in the pools
beside that temple, and wondered if they were still there.
Solange was sitting quietly in her corner of the cab, her
nose wrinkling involuntarily at the stench from some of
the side streets.

We got to better neighborhoods soon, went rolling past
mansions behind high fences, set in perfectly manicured
swards of lawn. *I had eaten Lucullan repasts in those*
houses during a forgotten war and stepped over the
bloated corpses of starvation victims all the way home.
They were dying at the rate of 4,000 a day in Calcutta
alone and couldn't be gathered up and burned fast enough
. . .

We went down Chowringee Road, Lower Circular
Lane, and came finally to Rainey Park, a minor mansion
set among its own trees and rolling lawns. The Sikh driver
jackknifed out and put his head in the back window.
These gentlemen never cut their hair, and he had greasy
black strands curling out from under his head wrapping.

"The person you wish to see, sahib, is?" he asked.

"General Sir Lal Bahadur Singh!" I said, perhaps too
fiercely. If you can avoid a touch of asperity with a name
like that, you are not normal.

"Tik hai!" The Sikh driver turned away from us and

rattled the locked iron gates. Nobody came, so he returned and honked the horn endlessly. Solange giggled. The Sikh returned to the gates and shook them again, and a weary sigh came out of the small gate lodge. A small brown man came to stand behind the barred entrance, one hand jerking up his dirty dhoti and the other knuckling his eyes.

"A master come to see the General Sir Lal Bahadur Singh, so open the gate, you piece of shit," said the Sikh in Urdu. The sleepy little man groped back to his lodge and came back with an enormous iron key. It had only two teeth in it, and you could have opened the gates with a Popsicle stick, but he made a production out of it. And why not? That was what he did in life. He opened the gates at the house of General Sir Lal Bahadur Singh.

The Sikh would have powerhoused his cab right up the curving gravel drive to the darkhouse, but I made him stop when we were just inside the gates. I handed a ten-rupee note to the gatekeeper, who made a deep obeisance. He hadn't expected it, and would have gone back to sleep in his lodge well content without it. My conscience was the thing being bought off; the chill wind of famine was blowing across India again, and I was so thankful that I didn't have to stay and walk over corpses again that I ponied up.

There were candles glowing in the main hallway of the big house, beyond the wide veranda. A bearer clad in spotless white came down the steps and made the *namaste* sign of steepled hands beside our taxi. I said that I was Captain Mallory, head of Civil Aviation in Burma, and had just made a special flight to see the general. I apologized for the inconvenient hour, and asked him to see if the general would receive us.

"Yes, please," said the bearer, and opened the taxi door. "You will enter, isn't it?"

Solange and I followed him up the few steps, across the wide veranda, and were ushered into an enormous sitting room. The bearer was rustling ahead in his starched white uniform, bare feet noiseless, and he switched on two lamps. "Please be seated," he said, "and I will awaken the general."

Solange and I sat on the carved ebony chairs and considered each other. Travel-worn, we were. Lights flashed down the circular stairwell in the hall, and the bearer came back to the entrance of the sitting room. He was smiling. "I will fix tea," he said. "The general will be here soon."

Singh came down the stairway with a deliberate tread, which was not surprising because he was over eighty years old. He was a fierce-looking old man, with sun-cured mahogany skin and spiky, upturned white mustachios. Tucking at the belt of his brocaded dressing gown, he approached us like a proud-nosed Punch now out of service, and we both arose. When he saw Solange, his grim features relaxed, and he went to her first.

"My dear, I didn't know, or else I would have dressed more suitably. What is your name?"

"Solange LeBlanc, General," she said, and he nodded. The tips of his white mustachios were almost quivering, as though he could remember many charming young ladies like Solange put efficiently to bed. *My God*, I thought with involuntary admiration, *the old swordsman is turned on* ... Sir Lal Bahadur had once been commanding general of His Majesty's Own Assamese Rifles, with four battalions of Gurkhas attached. One of the few Indian generals to serve under the British, he had been respected by all ranks.

He turned to me. "Your presence is somewhat mitigated, Captain Mallory, by the company you keep. I hope your business is important enough to warrant an invasion of my privacy."

"I hope so, too, General," I said. The bearer came gliding in with an enormous tray loaded with a tea service and set it down deftly on the low teak table. Willy-nilly, we all had a cuppa, and crumpets, and odd lots of biscuits. I slugged my cup with lemon, drank half of it, and asked if Solange could retire. To the garden, perhaps. Dawn was graying through the windows, across the wide

117

veranda, silhouetting the broad leaves of the banyan trees.

The general stared at me over the wafer-thin edge of his Meissen cup. "You are an impatient man, sir," he said. "Why did you bring the lady if she cannot be privy to your message?"

"She is very dear to me, sir. But what I have to say is a security matter."

That did it. "Security." It locks up the military types. He escorted Solange into the brightening garden, and the bearer went after them with the tea tray.

When the general came back in to sit across from me, he was no longer the octogenarian courtier. "All right," he said curtly.

I outlined the position for him, right down to the nut-cutting, because this was not a man you lied to. I said that I had served in War Two, with CNAC, on the Hump for three years. That I had met him in Tezpur just before the Chindit invasion of Burma. That I was a contract agent in counterintelligence for the United States, and that I had been assigned to rid Burma of the remnants of the renegade Nationalist Division, which had been in upper Burma for many years.

What I wanted, I explained, was the *sub rosa* recruitment of a Gurkha battalion, to be flown from the abandoned airstrip in Sukrating, Upper Assam, to Man Hpang in the Shan States, in Burma. Leaning forward with my hands dangling between my knees, I told the Indian ex-general that I knew he was a commander that the Gurkhas swore by, under blood oath. That I had seen the spindly-legged little warriors in the tapered-brim hats raise their crooked kukris to him in parade in a way they had never done to any European officer.

The general took all this applesauce in stride, as he had taken so much other applesauce in his long military career. "Give me one of your cigars," he said, and I handed him one of the green cheroots. He had his original teeth, except for a few gaps, and he snapped the tip off the cigar. I lighted it.

"You talk about a battalion, Captain Mallory. In one

day, even with Gurkhas, you plan to land them, over-whelm the remnant of a division, and remove them from Burmese soil that same day or the next. Is that right?"

"Yes, sir. I have been in Man Hpang twice and seen how sloppy the troops keep there."

The old eyes narrowed behind the cheroot. "You have been in their camp twice?"

"Yes, sir." I held up the nub of my amputated finger. "First time, they took my plane away and got this much of me. Second time, I parachuted in, a few days later, and attached magnetic beacons to every frigging plane on their flight line."

General Singh expelled a cloud of cigar smoke. "I like that, sir! I like that very much!" And I knew I had him. He pontificated awhile longer, said it would take some time, and quoted me an approximate price. I cut the time in half and offered him twice the money. He rubbed his seamed chin, and growled that it might be possible. But that if the scheme backfired, it would cause serious international repercussions, and that he would swear he had never heard anything about it.

I tilted the price a little more, which put it near to 700,000 U.S. dollars, and he nodded and agreed to let me know in three days. He stressed that the Gurkhas, mercenary all their history, required payment in advance, but promised me that they would never fault the jump. We walked into the garden toward Solange, a graceful figure on a stone bench. She had scattered crumbs from her tea cakes on the far end of the bench, and a scarlet bulbul with a black beak was pecking at them busily . . .

When we had shaken the Sikh cab driver awake, he snorted up behind the wheel, and we went back down the curving gravel drive. Behind us General Singh was waving good-bye from the veranda. It was full daylight, so I took Solange to breakfast in the Great Eastern Hotel. We were served very light, flaky hot cakes bathed in honey, and around our table I heard exactly the same clipped British complaints that I had heard so many years ago. Only now they were being voiced by upper-class Indians who seemed no different, except that they had better tans.

Sitting there, listening to the querulous gossip, I wondered what Mohandas Karamchand Gandhi, the Bapu, would have thought of them.

SINCE NO ANSWER from General Singh could be expected for several days, I busied myself with a complete overhaul of the Burmese civil aviation fleet. Sunby, Gardella, and I, after placing a suitable amount of baksheesh in Upper Assam, flew nine drum-loads of high-octane fuel into the abandoned airstrip at Sukrating. Night after night I charted the logistics and pilot demands on the surprise airlift of an entire battalion. And their return to the anonymous base.

Finally it was all done. We had the planes ready; we had the palms greased, and no obvious hitch appeared on either side of the Indian-Burmese border. This was mostly because the operation, if it came off, would involve very sparsely populated areas. In short, we had everything but the Gurkha battalion, so we waited.

I was still concerned with the Chiangmai trips from Man Hpang and decided to find out what they actually were. On a Monday, Sunby, Gardella, and I all piled into one of the Doves two hours before dawn and were over Man Hpang before the Nationalist fleet took off. We locked onto one of the Chiangmai-bound planes after its course was set, and when it landed on the remote dirt strip in northwest Thailand, we were right behind it.

A six-wheeler truck had begun to pull out of the wooded area to unload the incoming plane, but when its driver saw the three of us jump out of the Dove and advance with leveled weapons, he roared around in a tight turn and went bouncing back into the forest.

We had fanned out as we approached the renegade lightplane, and one of the Chinese pilots leaned out and fired an automatic pistol at us. That was so ineffably stupid that I tripped the hip-held BAR and stitched the windshield of the pilot's enclosure back and forth. What we got then was impressive silence.

While the three of us stood surrounding the plane, the Chinese pilots scrambled out with their hands high. Gardella herded them to one side with his carbine, and Sunby and I shook the plane down. It was loaded to capacity with gray balls of crude opium, about grapefruit size. We put them in the Dove, and before we got through with the transfer, I calculated they must represent several million U.S. dollars, even in their unrefined form.

When the opium was loaded, we hustled the Chinese pilots aboard the Dove, ripped the magneto and generator out of the Chinese plane, and took off for Bangkok. It was a beautiful, cloudless day, and as we cruised along, Gardella sat in back with the two Chinese prisoners. Telling them that the U.S. had not yet unleashed its principal weapon in the Vietnamese War. Not hydrogen bombs, anything like that. *No, sir,* he explained, with great, swooshing arabesques of his hands, *we would soon be sending over Batman* . . .

The Chinese pilots knew just enough English to be puzzled; they listened with great attention to the tale of this avenging monster in black underwear. Beside me Sunby was, as always, listening to his plane's performance, but occasionally his eyebrows went up as Gardella threatened credulous Asia with Batman. Charley was flying the plane because he was the best pilot on board, and I just leaned back listening to Gardella and tried to be the best copilot.

We went into the Don Muang flight pattern late in the afternoon, landed routinely, and taxied over to the military hangar. I left Sunby and Gardella with the prisoners and caught a cab to the U.S. Embassy in downtown Bangkok. After a twenty-minute wait I got to see a third-stringer, a rather blasé one, and explained what I had in the Dove.

His eyes popped open, and I thought he might lose a button off his silk bush jacket. He excused himself, as if stricken with locked bowels, and in another minute came back in followed by a leathery Air Force colonel named Yates. Colonel Yates was hot as an exploding firecracker.

"Good Christ, Mallory!" he growled, "I know you're on some kind of black assignment. But man, don't you know this country has secret military airports all over it? You come flying in raggedy-assed over national boundaries from a neutral country and want the whole goddamned war to whang dead-stop while you—"

"Whoa, birdman!" I held up both hands, and that made the colonel so mad I thought he might pick his teeth with his Good Conduct badge. "My news is of vital interest to anybody fighting this war. Most of this Man Hpang fleet is kicking off contract rice to the Vietcong, and I've got at least two million dollars' worth of raw opium out in my plane now. Contraband opium. Plus the Chinese Nationalist pilots who flew it into Thailand from Burma. Do you help me?"

"Help you?" He was livid under his tan. "I'll help you by putting you under immediate arrest and stuffing you in a black hole marked 'file and forget.'"

I sighed. At last he had said something I could understand. The third-string diplomat was puke-colored, and wished to be elsewhere.

"Why don't you try that, Colonel?" I asked in a mild voice. "And when you take the first step toward it, I'll turn you inside out. That may be painful, too; those chickens on your soldiers may scratch considerably going up your ass."

Colonel Yates reached for his cigarette case. His hand was shaking badly, and his breath was labored. It was a nice case, silver with acid etchings of temple dancers on it. I watched him for a few seconds more, turned, and walked out of the embassy.

My next stop was at the English-language paper in Bangkok. The assistant editor, a fortyish gentleman named Halvorsen, heard me out impassively. He kept nodding and making notes on yellow copy paper. When I was finished, he shook his head and dropped his pencil. The smell of ink and hot metal was heavy; the building was backed up to one of the klongs, and the hubbub of passing boat traffic floated in through the rush of blue twilight.

"No secret about the opium traffic," the lanky editor said, and shifted his feet on the paper-crowded desk. "And most of it has been coming in through the Chiang-mai region. But I don't think they'll let us print anything about it . . ."

"Couldn't you send a photographer and a reporter out to Don Muang, at least have it in your files?"

"No," said Halvorsen. "I don't think we could. You're a spook aren't you, Captain Mallory?"

"Yes," I said.

He nodded, then shook his head again. Took a nasal inhalator out of his pocket and sucked deeply at it through the left nostril. "What you really need," he went on, "is to talk to someone in the Thailand Defense Ministry?"

"That's right."

He reached for his phone and called three numbers. I didn't know the language, but all three calls were obviously disappointing. On the fourth he snagged somebody and growled out a few yards of maggoty Sibilanese. Hung up with a pleased half-smile.

"General Phari, number three in the Defense Ministry, will hear what you have to say, at his home. A great honor. He's doing it principally because he's an ambitious little bastard. Shrewd, though. Have you got a car?"

I said "no," and Halvorsen shouted, and a little brown man came into the office. I thanked the languid editor, and he said just to let him know how it all came out— if it did. That our life from womb to tomb was an inspiring thing, if we could just learn to live with adversity. He was a man I would liked to have depleted a bottle with, but there was no time. As I left he was screwing the inhalator back into his nose. The other side this time.

General Phari received me, but just barely. The little driver nursed his weak-eyed cab over many arching bridges over many canals, and the heady perfumes of Bangkok changed from spice to sewage to dew-dripping flowers. We finally stopped before a red-lacquered gate, and one half of it opened when the cab stopped.

A bowing servant took me not to the pagoda-styled pavilion house filled with lights but into a shadowed garden. General Phari was wearing a European suit and motioned for me to sit beside him on a stone bench, beside a splashing fountain. I told him the story, and he nodded, a handsome little brown man with a Sy Devore-type collar and dark tie. He smelled of good Scotch, taken frequently.

"It is a matter of great concern, Captain," he said, "if such shipments of opium, in tonnage amounts, are entering Thailand. This government would view it very gravely. I will bring it to the attention of the Defense Minister first thing in the morning . . ."

I was very tired. As General Phari's precisely inflected voice droned on I realized that it was really the splashing fountain I was hearing. He was talking in the muted tone of the United Nations—when the delegates are most polite, and most intent on lying to each other.

". . . will you be staying?" he was asking.

"At the airport hotel, General," I said wearily. "Thank you for talking to me."

I got up, and he escorted me back to the lacquered gate, murmuring what a terrible thing this opium business was. I bowed to him under the lantern light, noticing his pointed Italian shoes, and got back in the cab.

When I returned to Don Muang, the Dove was still parked on the apron before the military hangar, but it was empty. No Chinese prisoners, no cargo of opium. No Sunby or Gardella, either. I found them drinking coffee in the airport terminal. It seems that four cars of Thailand military intelligence officers, accompanied by an American colonel named Yates, had relieved us of all our worries.

Further, since we had entered Thailand without authorization, we had only two hours to remove ourselves and the Dove from its territorial boundaries. I ordered a sandwich and a cup of coffee while Sunby and Gardella watched me with disinterested interest. Three hours later we were back in Rangoon.

WHEN I WALKED back into the Strand Hotel lobby, seven cablegrams were waiting for me. After having had my requests ignored for so long, this largesse might have been pleasing ordinarily, but I knew something had ripped loose and I figured it might be me. One of the cables might even be my recall orders: fold the assignment and quit Burma.

I took the seven blue envelopes upstairs unopened and left them on my bed while I showered. While the cold water sluiced down over me I was thinking that it was my offering to manhandle that horse's ass Air Force colonel in Bangkok which had opened the communications sluice-gates. I had goofed badly, probably with a hotshot officer connected with our so-called "secret" airfields in Thailand . . .

That was it. One cable was from the State Department, another from the agency head, a third from the U.S. ambassador in Bangkok, and a fourth from Hong Kong station-chief Meyers. Taken all together, they represented considerable capsuled venom; I was to report this or that "soonest;" I had jeopardized our friendly relations with a leading neutral state; and I had been a disrupting factor in certain "tactical aspects" of the Vietnamese War. Benedict Arnold, it seemed, was a sneak-thief compared to me . . .

The other three cables were Washington acknowledgments of my previous requests. No high-altitude photography of Man Hpang would be possible, and the message was just that curt. Another said that in-depth dossiers on

Hal Pottschmidt, Harry Liu, Solange LeBlanc, and Will Michaels were being prepared. That was another kick, because I had shot Will Michaels to death some time ago, and Harry Liu had defected to the Man Hpang team. The final cable was from Meyers, Hong Kong, and said he had been unable to ascertain present whereabouts of Hal Pottschmidt. He had not been seen Hong Kong for some time. I swear to Christ the message said "ascertain;" also, the cable had been sent in the open, so that every station in Asia would be glad to tell Potts I was checking on him.

I had knotted a clean cotton lungyi around my waist and was combing my hair when Solange came in with a tall drink. Her eyes widened at the pile of blue papers and envelopes on my bed, and I thanked her for the drink and handed her the cable from Meyers. The one in the clear, about being unable to locate Pottschmidt.

She read it and sat down on the bed, not looking at me.

"Solange," I said slowly, "I made a bad mistake in Bangkok and, like President Johnson, I'm bogged down in the great land mass of Asia. Only he has more options than I have. I might get jerked out of Burma at any minute, or they might allow me to stay and get killed. Do you understand what I'm talking about?

"No," she said.

"Okay, I'll simplify it. You are working for me—and you are also working for Hal Pottschmidt. Now, I know the form; it's just a little more cumshaw, baksheesh, whatever. But I think Captain Pottschmidt will kill me, or have me killed, if I stay in Burma. And I think it will happen soon. So what's your pleasure, kid? Get on one side or the other."

Her head came up, and her eyes were filled with tears. She dropped the cable on the floor and got up. Shaking her head angrily and brushing at her eyes as she left the room.

My God, I thought! *That simple. A few tears, and she checks out . . .*

It wasn't that simple. I heard a drawer being jerked out

in her bedroom, and she came back to hand me a slip of stiff paper.

"I will leave whenever you wish me to," she said; her head was up, and the tears were gone. She looked adamant as any of Siva's jet-haired daughters.

The slip of paper was the voucher end of a bearer draft in the amount of Rupees 7,800—, drawn on the Rangoon branch of The Bank of India, Australia & China. I knew the bank and most of its officials; I had used their facilities in dealing with the Burmese treasury in my previous stay in the country.

"So?" I asked harshly. "Somebody, unnamed on this draft, has, or has cashed on sight, a bankable instrument in this amount."

"The date, please," she said, and I noticed it. "Before I came to the Peninsula Hotel in Hong Kong to apply for this job with you, Captain Potts gave me ten thousand Hong Kong dollars. He paid it to me so I would report what I could find out about your actions. As you say, Captain Mallory, this is not unusual. I have done it before."

"Okay, okay, so you sent him back his money. Why?"

Siva's daughter's dark eyes were blazing. "I returned it because he did try to kill you. On the day after Captain Michaels died, when they tried to trap you."

I checked back rapidly. The date on the stub was right, and I made the rough computation in my head. It came out at about $10,000 Hong Kong.

"Captain Koenig took the draft to him by safe hand," she said. "The same day I got it from the bank. Do you wish me to go?"

I knew Steve Koenig; he flew the Hong Kong-Bangkok-Rangoon-Calcutta leg for Cathay-Pacific Airways.

"What do you want to do, Solange?" I asked, and she walked straight into me and kissed me thoroughly.

"I want to stay with you," she said.

"All right," I said, and loosened her silk sari. It fell to the floor, and I tossed her, long legs kicking, into the middle of the bed. The cablegrams and their envelopes flew every which way, which expressed my opinion of them exactly. After we had loved an hour and slept two, I got up and went over the airlift plans again.

I got to sleep at dawn, and in midmorning Solange shook me awake. I came up hard, clawing at the loaded pistol under my pillow. Ever so gently she took it out of my hand, and called for William to bring in the coffee tray. Then she creamed and sugared two cups while I climbed down off the high wire.

"You have a visitor," she said. "From Calcutta."

My visitor was General Singh's bearer. He did not look as impressive in a European suit as in his starched whites and turban.

The Gurkha battalion would be standing ready, with full battle gear, on the Sukrating strip in three days. The battalion would have no support or engineering elements attached, but would be a purely combat force. One mortar company. The Gurkha soldiers would not leave Indian soil until after payment of the agreed amount to General Singh, in Calcutta.

T HIRTY-SIX HOURS BEFORE my small invasion force was to be airlifted from Upper Assam, the funds to pay the Gurkha mercenaries had not arrived. I had requested them immediately after I had learned the availability date of the battalion, and my request had been confirmed by Washington. The agency had advised that the bank notes, in Indian lakhs of rupees, would be sent by courier from New Delhi to the U.S. Rangoon Embassy, addressed to me.

My Bangkok caper was rapidly turning into a *cause*

célèbre in papers all over Asia. News of Thailand's confiscation of the ton of raw opium and its two Chinese pilot-smugglers was bound to break over to the European and U.S. press, and I knew if they played it up, I was odd man out, my mission aborted.

With less than a day and a half left I checked the embassy again and got the same result. Stony indifference. No, no parcel or message had come through from New Delhi for me in the diplomatic pouch. It was obvious that the striped pants set was going to give me a rough hustle.

After waiting until eleven that night, I called General Ne Win on the unlisted number at his home. He answered the phone himself, as he had done the other time, and I said I had to see him immediately. Could I come to his house?

"No," said the general. "At the War Office. I will be there in twenty minutes."

My cab arrived at the heavily barricaded building at the same time as Ne Win's chauffeur-driven Rolls, and the stocky little man nodded to the rigid sentries and walked me by the rolls of barbed wire and into the War Office, our footsteps echoing along the darkened corridors.

The general sat behind his desk and listened impassively to my tale of woe. The nonarrival of the fee for the Gurkha battalion. He was in civilian clothes, sitting erect with his thumbs hooked into his vest pockets. When I had finished, he nodded.

"You have stirred up considerable trouble, Captain Mallory," he commented, "since I saw you last."

"You mean the Bangkok business?"

"Yes."

"That may have been a bad blunder on my part—" I began, but Ne Win held up one hand.

"I do not mind the publicity," he said. "We have been telling Burma's side of this sorry tale for years. Then you arrive and confront the authorities in Thailand with the facts of the matter. Those immaculate gentlemen, with U.S. assistance, hurriedly brush the evidence under the rug. No, I do not mind."

"But, sir, if I don't have the Gurkha payment in Calcutta tomorrow, that battalion won't budge the next day. And my people are almost sure to jerk me out of Burma when the clamor mounts in the States."

"I see." The general meditated. "Unfortunately I cannot withdraw that much foreign exchange from our treasury without inviting comment. Does your agency guarantee ultimate payment of this fee to the Gurkha troops?"

"Yes, sir," I said, because I was gambling at the front table now. I had to believe what I said was true. It was either that or go back to the hotel, pack my bags, and leave Burma.

"Then, follow me, please." Ne Win arose, and I followed him down the main hallway and a stairway into the basement of the War Office building. At the entrance to a bank-style crypt two sentries challenged us sharply and then snapped to attention as they recognized the dictator. He returned their salutes idly, opened another door, and spun three combination dials on a huge, circular steel door. When we were inside the vault, he opened six small leather trunks.

They were filled to brimming with enormous matched rubies of pigeon's-blood hue. They were star rubies of the finest quality. Under the pale glare of the overhead bulb, in the chilled air of the vault, they were a fantastic display of deep red stars. Not many men, in all their lives, get to see such a sight. I crouched and touched a few of the tremendous rubies; they were icy.

Above me General Win was smiling slightly. "Yes," he said, "they are impressive, aren't they? Burmese State Treasures, collected through the centuries from our mines in Mogok. King stones, every one. Harry Winston, your famous jeweler, was in this country three years ago and offered us four million dollars for these rubies. I told him they did not belong on the shriveled necks and fingers of Western dowagers . . . Who do you take them to?"

I stood up. "General Lal Singh, in Calcutta."

"I know him. He is an honorable man. Tell him these stones are surety only, for paying the Gurkhas. They are worth far more than the fee. When do you send them to him?"

"At daylight, sir. Captain Sunby will fly them there and deliver them personally. In one of our Dakotas, with an armed guard of eight crewmen."

The dictator nodded. "All right. Major Ferrara will deliver the trunks to the aerodrome at dawn and go with Captain Sunby to make delivery."

"Yes, sir," I said. "Thank you."

Ne Win nodded again and asked me to wait in his office until fifteen minutes after his car had left. A cab would be sent to pick me up at the barricaded gate.

Sunby took off from Rangoon with the caskets of rubies an hour after dawn, and I spent the rest of the morning getting the planes in the ferry fleet ready to leave for Upper Assam. We were on a very tight schedule because the planes had to land at Sukrating strip that same day; it had no night facilities, no beacons or landing lights. And since our Doves couldn't make Sukrating nonstop, I had to send them on in the morning to refuel at Mandalay.

Sunby was back by noon and reported safe delivery of the jewels. Major Ferrara had stayed behind to assist General Singh in putting them up on a short-term loan to raise money for the Gurkha fee. So Sunby, Solange, and I had a drink together in the suite; the way seemed open for our airlift. Charley went back to the aerodrome to check his Dakota, and I was giving Solange last-minute instructions when William came in and handed me a cable.

It was from Calcutta, from the U.S. Consul-General there, and I was gratified to think State was cooperating, finally, until I decoded it.

The message said that the house of Sir Lal Bahadur Singh had been invaded by dacoits an hour ago. Singh, his aide, a Burmese major named Ferrara, and six servants had been slaughtered, and the house ransacked. Signed: *A. Saunders, Consul-General.*

My gut began cramping. Solange glanced at me, saw my stricken look, and brought me a big drink. I tasted it automatically. The time sequence was a big thing; the sending time on the Calcutta cable was about five hours after Sunby had landed there. Had General Singh and Major Ferrara had time to make the bank loan and notify the force in Sukrating? If the State Treasure of star rubies had been stolen by the "dacoits," I was out of business. The battalion in Upper Assam would never board my planes.

I had no choice, no time to check Calcutta for further details. The whole operation was about to collapse under me, and my only hope was to check my planes at Mandalay and Sukrating. *To see if, in some unforeseeable way, I could get the operation off on schedule.* While I got into my flying clothes Solange watched in silence. She was wearing a white Benares sari spangled with moons and stars worked in silver thread, and her dark face was scrubbed clean.

After I had checked and hefted the case with the BAR in it, she answered my kiss and tucked a letter into my jacket pocket. Said I was not to read it until I was in the air, and I nodded.

"I love you, Joseph," she said, and I frowned in annoyance. *Another specter at the feast,* because our arrangement had worked very well without any mention of love . . . She smiled faintly and added, "Good luck."

"May need it, Light of Asia," I answered, and walked out of the suite and down the hall. The station wagon was waiting at the side entrance of the Strand, and I got in beside the driver. Traffic was heavy, and we moved along through it, past traffic policemen semaphoring wildly with white elbow-length gloves. We were stopping for the fourth time, almost even with the towering Shwe Dagon Pagoda, when a voice spoke in English at my elbow.

"Sir Spook rides again, eh?" asked the voice, and I turned toward the crowded sidewalk. A tall man stepped closer. "Remember me?" he asked.

I nodded. He was Halvorsen, the American editor of the Bangkok English-language paper. The one who had arranged the nothing interview for me just before I got thrown out of Thailand.

"If you could spare a couple of minutes," said Halvorsen politely, "I've got a friend who would like to talk to you."

I stared at him. The traffic ahead of us had moved on, and my station wagon was holding up the vehicles behind. Horns were braying and tooting, angry voices were shouting, and the enraged policeman ahead was semaphoring so wildly that he seemed about to fly right out of his intersection stand. My driver was becoming overheated, too, racing the engine.

"Park on the other side and wait," I told him, and stepped out of the station wagon. Halvorsen went plunging through the crowd toward the huge pagoda, and I followed him. We left our shoes at the entrance to the temple, tipping the bonze in charge, and I followed the editor around the first circular passage inside. We passed bells of all sizes, hung on beams and strung from poles, and saw pilgrims clanging on them with deer antlers. This was to call attention to their piety in making offerings to Lord Gautama.

Almost completely across the pagoda, Halvorsen turned into a recessed doorway that led to one of the monks' offices and quarters. These small, dark rooms ringed the exterior of the Shwe Dagon and could be entered from either outside or inside the temple. I opened the flap on my holster and followed Halvorsen. The smell of wilted flowers and unwashed bodies was everywhere, spiced by the more acrid odors of betel and pan.

The room was dim; the outer door was closed. While my eyes were coming back to focus in the gloom, the editor stepped past me, back inside the temple. He closed the door, and it was darker than ever. A tic started jerking in my right cheek, and I had my hand on the pistol butt when something scraped. A dim figure moved, and a lamp was lighted.

A hump-shouldered Buddhist monk in a saffron robe was sitting across the room on a mat. His head was shaved and his fingers steepled as he considered me serenely. The bulky legs were crossed in the lotus position but showed

133

no strain. Outside on the busy street, traffic roared along, and bells kept clanging inside the pagoda.

"Well, old friend," said the seated figure, "here we are again . . ."

Then, but not until then, did I realize that the yellow-robed monk was Hal Pottschmidt. When I did not answer, only took my right hand off the pistol and clamped down on the nerve throbbing in my cheek, Potts laughed softly.

"You're surprised, Joe? Shouldn't be. It's not just a costume I put on." He stared at the tiny flame of the lamp, and it was twin-mirrored in his eyes. "After you went home, after all of you went home from the big rock-candy mountains after War the Second, I had plenty of money. Stayed in Hong Kong and started a couple of airlines, played big-shot taipan. Then that became a drag, so I tried Buddhism, really tried it. Went begging up and down Burmese roads with my own bowl for a year. Tried to become a guru. But it didn't work . . ."

I sat down on the floor, still pressing my cheek. The worn bricks were immaculate.

". . . went back Stateside once or twice a year to keep from going Asiatic, but I couldn't understand what those people were doing. I didn't fit there, and finally didn't seem to fit anywhere . . ."

I grunted. "There was a time, Potts, when every pilot in Asia wanted to ride copilot to you. You were the best navigator in the world."

The reflective monk shrugged his heavy shoulders. "You can't navigate all your life, Joe. So I made arrangements to move to Switzerland next year; the accounts are arranged and the villa bought. And then, after I spend eighteen years setting up the big operation, you arrive. Just before the payoff. Kid, you're about to tear up my pea patch."

"I didn't know it was yours, Potts. I go where they send me."

"Sure, Joe." The massive, shaved head turned from the lamp flame toward me. "But I've spent a long time paying the cumshaw, taking the shake. Setting up the Yünan-

134

Man Hpang-Chiangmai opium route. And in the last few years our rice kickoffs to Vietnam have also become big business. So you see, old friend, I can't let your little ragged-ass fleet haul those Gurkhas into Man Hpang tomorrow morning. It would put me out of business."

I shook my head. "Potts, I know you're a businessman. But doesn't the morality of your opium hustle and the fact that you are supplying the Vietcong, who are killing Americans after you fill their bellies, make any difference to you?"

"Not much," he said. "We had the same dubious morality in the earlier war, and got sold out." Deftly, without touching the floor with his hands, he stood erect. I got up to face him. "You can't get the Gurkhas to move anyway. You've nothing to pay them with."

I could smell fear coming out of Pottschmidt. We stood a few feet apart, knowing there was no help for what was coming. And that was a shame, because once when the world was young, Potts *had* been the standard of excellence to which all young pilots wished to aspire. His name had been a legend from Karachi to Tsingtao. Now the big shoulders were sagging. He was heavily dewlapped, and livid scars that would never tan snaked across his big head and down the sides of his neck. They were the scars he had suffered when I had dragged him out of the burning plane in Kunming. He saw my eyes flicker and nodded. "Aye, Joe, it's late now. We're in too deep."

"That's right, Potts."

He pushed his weathered hands loose from the yellow sleeves and studied them. "If it happened again today, Joe, would you still pull me out of burning wreckage?"

"I don't think so, Potts," I said, trying to be honest. "I didn't hesitate, didn't think, then. Today I'd think, because I've picked up a few scars myself."

"Too right, kid," agreed the muscular bogus monk. "So do me a favor. Don't go to Sukrating, and I'll deliver those rubies to you within an hour. At your hotel here in Rangoon."

"I can't do that, Potts," I said regretfully. Knowing he had never meant for me to leave the pagoda alive.

135

"Then, Joe, a few U.S. bombers will clobber your little flying circus in the morning before it can leave for Man Hpang. One of those unfortunate errors, where the planes leave Thailand, fly the wrong way and have to jettison their loads. And it will happen with the knowledge and consent of Colonel Yates in Bangkok. He hates your guts."

I nodded, flipped the top off the small gas container in my jacket pocket, and threw the spewing capsule in his face. Potts saw it coming but had taken a breath or two before he reacted, and so he slumped to his knees, coughing and clawing at his face.

I tugged once at the inner door, and shot the lock out. The boom of the Magnum .357 nearly ruptured my bad eardrum again, and then I was inside the pagoda.

Two men fired at me from the shadowed corridor, but I had gone diving across it, and they missed. Pilgrims began shouting and fleeing down the rounded hall. Snapping off shots from the hand cannon as I lunged, I saw the face of one would-be assassin turn to tomato surprise, but the other dropped behind one of the stone tables piled with offerings of fruit and flowers. I rolled on one shoulder, came up running, and snatched a set of deer antlers with my left hand.

Flailing and herding at the fleeing pilgrims with the antlers, I kept the gun hand ready. Sure enough, the other gunman took a peek, and it cost him the top of his head. I ran on, still lashing with the antlers, out of the pagoda. The station wagon was parked across the street, and my driver was draped out the window, chatting with passersby. When I clanged the deer antlers just behind him, he cranked up. I dived in beside him, and we rolled away.

He did a nice job of removing us from the area because I had the pistol muzzle in his left ear, and its barrel was still hot.

"We go to Mingaladon Aerodrome now, chop-chop," I said, and the driver nodded vigorously. People will do almost anything if you just reason with them.

AN HOUR LATER, I was trimming up *X-Ray* as we flew northwest. When we were at 15,000 feet, on the autopilot, I considered the position. It wasn't good. There was no money to pay the Gurkha troops, and if Potts could be believed, there wasn't even any reason to pay them. I felt inclined to believe his story that a few U.S. bombers from the "secret" bases in Thailand would knock out Sukrating strip in the morning, with all my planes on it. Potts had been in the Far East a long time and was probably hooked up with some U.S. agency, perhaps the same one I was under contract to.

Sitting with my hand on the yoke, feeling the vibration of the plane through it, I remembered the note Solange had stuck into my pocket. I took it out, ripped open the envelope, and read it.

"Joseph, I think I am carrying your child. You are not to worry, or get angry about this, because I quit taking the pills some time ago. After the night in Hong Kong, to be exact, when you explained how women can have injections to make their breasts bigger. You did that nicely, not laughing at me or making it a dirty thing, and for the first time in my life I felt that a man had made love to me as a person. As Solange, not an object to try different sex techniques on . . .

I looked up and frowned. Tin, the Burmese copilot, wanted to go to the can, and I nodded and watched him inch out into the corridor and go back through the plane. The even thunder of the engines went on.

Many men have done things to me, and we both know that after you have finished your job in

Burma, you will take me back to Hong Kong and leave me there. So what I had to look forward to, after you left your Eurasian playmate, was more men. Until I was too old to please them. I decided to keep something of you. I hope it turns out to be a small boy. Because, even if he has a touch of the Hanoi tar-brush from me, I will have another lover. In a different way, until he gets old enough to be ashamed of me.

Solange LeBlanc

I cracked the side window and threw the note into the slipstream. It would land somewhere in Burma. Like Solange, it would be a part of the great Asian turbulence ... Blown about ...

The plane began to buck into head winds, and I took it off the pilot. The afternoon was waning below our wings, shadowing the Burmese terrain.

. . *How will I explain to General Ne Win about the loss of the State Treasures?* I wondered. And then, as the plane thundered on toward Upper Assam ... *that bitch cannot possibly know she is pregnant; she can't have missed more than one period* ...

Tin was back in the copilot's seat. I nodded at him, and when he took the controls, I eased out into the corridor and went balancing back through the cabin stripped for troop-carrying. The toilet compartment was cold, and the alclad sides of it chilled my hands as I leaned over the metal bowl and urinated. Vibration was in my hands and under my feet, and a sprung plate hummed.

Leaning there with my bladder draining, I thought of Solange's note, which I had cast to the winds. And something else, from an old speech of an unrepentant American Indian chief. *There runs not a drop of my blood in the veins of any living creature* ...

That was true of me, too. The thought that Solange might really be pregnant left me half-vexed and half-proud. But whether it was true or not, I thought as I zipped up my fly, she probably needed some kind of guard. Pottschmidt was ready to stack things up; he had had a look of blind fury when I left him in the pagoda

138

and he might strike at her simply because I was not available.

When I was back in the cockpit, I told the radio operator to get Radio Rangoon on the voice channel. When they were on, I requested that a 24-hour guard be put on my Strand Hotel suite, and that Miss LeBlanc not be allowed to leave it without an armed escort. Radio Rangoon said they would pass the message to the Office of Q Movements immediately and clicked off the air.

We sat in the dimly lighted pilot's enclosure and listened to the even thunder of the unseen engines outside in the darkness. Fifty minutes later Radio Rangoon came back on the air with our call signal, and I answered and told them to say on.

"Miss LeBlanc is not in the Strand Hotel suite, and all her effects have been removed," said Radio Rangoon in precisely accented English. "We are trying to determine when she left and her present whereabouts. Do you read?"

"Yes," I said. "Read you five and five. Please keep me informed. This is *X-Ray* over and out."

Then I hung the mike up and felt the acid break loose in my gut, gnawing at my vitals. I had been too late again. Tin, the little Burmese copilot, was looking at my face, so I changed it and gave him one of the twisted cheroots.

WE CAME TO Sukrating at the end of afternoon, and as we circled over the airstrip in deepening twilight I could see our lightplane fleet and the military Dakotas we had commandeered parked on the revetments below. From 8,000 feet, as Sunby took his plane down in a steep approach, I could see Tinsukia strip, Dinjan's hard-surfaced runways in Balijan District, and Dibrugarh on

139

the Brahmaputra River. Chabua should have been there, too, but I could not see it through the lengthening shadows.

When we could, we had flown down on the deck enroute, thundering over miles of Flame-of-The-Forest trees, flung across the Assamese valleys in riotous orange-scarlet splendor. The racket of our passage had startled grazing elephant herds into ponderous flight, trunks thrown up as they wheeled away. That signaled the passage of time, too, because during the Hump Operation in War Two those herds had grown so accustomed to aircraft that they wouldn't even stop swaying as we went over.

Sunby landed, pulled off the end of the strip, and gave Gardella and me landing instructions. And, when we were down, taxi and parking instructions. When I had locked the right brake and powered *X-Ray*'s tail around, I cut the switches gratefully, unstrapped myself, and eased out into the aisle. There, with my arms behind my back, I bowed forward and heard several vertebrae unlock like popping castanets.

The Gurkha battalion was bivouacked on the plain just south of the airstrip. Their tents made black angles in the dusk, and cheerful campfires flickered up and down the line, surrounded by crouching figures. Gardella and Sunby came over to join me, and we stood smoking and watching coolies swarm off the petrol truck I had sent over from Dibrugarh. Their flashlights probed, and they chattered constantly, squatting nearly naked on the wings as they fueled the Dakotas.

I stood staring past their torchlights at the fading outlines of the tea gardens surrounding the airfield. *Remembering the immaculately tended rows, jackals slinking through them at night, their eyes like yellow slits . . .*

The night I had stopped my jeep when a tremendous male tiger had leaped out on the road before me. Landed with cushioned ease and swung his great striped head at the jeep's headlight, eyes blazing orange. I had cut my headlights quickly because Shere Khan had the right-of-way there. The forest was his, the tea gardens, even the pretentious roads. I had been the intruder, and The Lord of That Place had flowed on across the road silently as heat ...

Sunby left us when the petrol truck pulled away from *X-Ray* and approached his plane, *Yoke*. No nearly naked wogs were going to scramble over his plane, like a bunch of monkeys, unless he knew exactly what they were doing with those hoses.

Gardella dropped his cigarette butt and toed its glowing ash with a flight boot. "Well, pappy," he said, "we're close to it now."

"Yes," I answered. "Would you do me a favor? Go over to the Gurkha camp and ask their commanding officer to come see me."

"Chop-chop," said Danny. "After that, we have a drink?"

"Several," I said, and the feisty little bantam nodded and went away whistling. In a few minutes he came back with a small, mahogany-colored man. Ramrod straight, wearing high-topped military shoes, long khaki shorts, and the distinctive flaring Gurkha campaign hat, front brim pinned back at an angle.

"Captain Mallory," said Gardella, "Leftn't-Colonel Janakpur."

The spindly-legged little man clapped his heels together, and whanged me off a flat-handed British salute. It was catching, so I bladed him off a Marine Corps type in return and told him to stand easy. That I was a civilian. His obsidian eyes flickered, as if to say: who sends a *civilian-wallah* to command an invasion? So I had to add that I had once been an officer, and he nodded politely and stood easier. When I asked him to follow me into the plane, he climbed the little metal ladder without question.

I turned on only the instrument lights, and sat in the left-hand seat. Colonel Janakpur eased himself cautiously into the copilot's seat, and we sat staring over the faint illumination from the clocks and dials, along the flight line. And beyond it the cheerful Gurkha campfires.

He turned in question when I told him that General

141

Singh, his former commanding officer, had been murdered by dacoits in his Calcutta home, and that we did not know if the collection of jewels had been banked before he met his death. If they had not, no payment for the services of his Gurkhas had been arranged.

Colonel Janakpur's face was stained pale violet by the glow from the instrument panel. "I do not know you, sir," he said simply. "General Singh asked us to come here. Now you say he is dead. Dead today. Who do we fight for, then, and who pays us?"

"I will guarantee the payment," I said. "And because the fee was delayed, I will add two lakhs of rupees to it."

"I do not know you, sir. Who is it you represent?" asked the Gurkha officer.

"A secret agency of the United States," I said.

"Oh?" His tone was skeptical now. "All people know how General Ne Win hates the United States. Why should they help him?"

"Because one day, not too distant from now, the United States and China will fight each other. When that happens, my country would like for Burma to be on our side, or at least to stay neutral."

Colonel Janakpur did not answer.

"There is another problem—a severe one," I continued. "My planes and your men cannot even stay here overnight. At dawn, before the time we had planned to take off for Man Hpang, this airstrip might be reduced to rubble by U.S. bombers."

Janakpur glanced at me. "Oh?"

"Yes."

"You do have problems," said the little brown man, without emotion. "You hire a mercenary battalion, uproot eight hundred lives, and then cannot pay for their services. You are a secret agent, you say, and then tell me that your own country's planes are about to destroy your unpaid assault force before it gets off the ground. A very odd way to fight a war, Captain."

"It is," I admitted wearily. "It is indeed. A question of

... conflicting opinions in high places. That and some enemies I made thoughtlessly."

Janakpur fell silent again, and I waited. There was no point in trying to con him; the alert officer had brought his superb fighting men a long way, and I had failed him.

"Look, Colonel," I said finally, "whatever happens, we must clear out of Sukrating in the next few hours. If you don't feel like committing your men on my unsupported word, we will load them up and fly them out in two hours. As soon as they can be loaded on the planes. And we will ferry them to any big airport in India or Nepal."

"It is not that simple, Captain Mallory!" Janakpur snapped. "You cannot simply unload a fully armed freelance battalion at any big airport. There are laws against it. If I should decide to have my men follow you in spite of these problems, what would happen?"

"We load the planes with your men and their gear as soon as possible, fly to Mandalay, and stay there until dawn. Then take off for Man Hpang, as planned."

"Won't your bombers see that we are gone from here and look for us elsewhere?"

"My God, no! They would never bomb anything inside Burma, and their attack will be at high altitude. I flew out of these fields during World War Two; they are nearly always overcast at dawn and often have ground fog."

Colonel Janakpur nodded, looking bleak, like a man who is making Hobson's Choice. "And if we pack and go to Mandalay, and on to Man Hpang in the morning, when will payment be made?" I started to answer, and he held up a warning hand. "Please, Captain Mallory, don't give me your country's word of honor. I won't accept it. Great states have no honor. Give me your personal word, just as I took General Singh's when I assembled these troops and brought them here."

The Gurkha colonel was only a welterweight, but he hit like a heavy.

"If your men go into Man Hpang as planned, I will fly

you directly to Rangoon after we have invested the Chinese camp. And put the cash agreed, plus two lakhs of rupees, into your hand. Then one of our planes will fly you to any destination you choose in India or Nepal."

"I see." He nodded. "There is also the matter of getting my troops out of Burma, back into India. If this airstrip is destroyed, my logistics of withdrawal are no good at all. Where do we come back to?"

"That one is easier," I said. "We return them to Dinjan Aerodrome, in Balijan District, only eighteen miles from here. A much larger and safer field, with a rail link to Dibrugarh and the Brahmaputra River."

Janakpur took off his slanted hat and ran nervous fingers through wiry black hair. "We will go with you, Captain Mallory. I do not like the situation, but I think you are an honest man. And I hope you are an honorable one."

"Thank you, Colonel," I said, and snapped off the pale violet light on the instrument panel. We went back through the stripped cabin of the plane and shook hands briefly on the ground. The little officer said his battalion would have its camp struck and be ready to enplane in two hours. Then he flashed me the jerky salute again and walked toward the campfires.

Sukrating was a madhouse for those two hours. Since the strip had no runway lights, I had to position planes along both sides of it. On call from my transmitter in *X-Ray* they loaded, fired up their fans, and as I called them out, took off in the flood of landing lights from the other planes. I was last off, with seventy little brown soldiers in the cabin behind me, and of course there were no guide lights left except two campfires winking at the far end of the runway.

. . *When you have to do it, you do it*. I applied full power, let her roll until the mercury-pull was dangerously high, and hauled *X-Ray* up into the dark and starless sky.

AFTER FERRYING HIS load of Gurkhas to Mandalay, Charley Sunby had flown back empty to Chabua, where the field would furnish lights on demand. He had taken off from Chabua again just before dawn and been stooging around Sukrating, well out of range, when the heavy bombers came across from Thailand and released their loads at 50,000 feet through the overcast by radar. They were precisely on target, he reported to me later in Mandalay, and the abandoned airstrip at Sukrating was turned into a smoking ruin.

Our invasion of Man Hpang was without incident. Although it would seem dangerous to send 800 men against an entrenched division and airfield, there were many factors which reduced the danger. First, although General Pao had entered the Shan States in full divisional strength, plus his air force, many debilitating years had gone by. I had seen that his troops lived like pigs and observed little discipline. His enclave force had degenerated into little more than a corps.

With the Man Hpang fleet gone on its opium and rice-supply missions, our planes came at the field shortly after ten in the morning. We approached at treetop level, so low that the antiaircraft guns had no traverse at us, and the sporadic ground fire was of small caliber. We had, of course, the element of surprise, and four of our planes were down and unloading before the first hostile fire began.

Even while the planes were slowing down, the Gurkhas hit the ground running, fanned out into the lines of skirmishers for which they were famous, and sealed off the operations office, the tower, and the hangars with a brisk, staccato fire. Only one Dove was hit, and it crumpled on a wing, ground-looped, and knobby-kneed little brown men

145

came crawling out of it and massacred the antiaircraft gunners and the sentries beside the helicopters.

By noon the airport, barracks, and warehouses had been flushed completely, to the stitching cough of automatic weapons. General Pao's bungalow down the road had been surrounded, and the huge General captured, together with his entire staff except for a few patriots who now littered his house and garden.

Before one in the afternoon all prisoners were confined in the warehouses, and Colonel Janakpur came back to my Dakota to report that resistance was at an end. His men had placed sentries on the road and at all possible approach points to the airfield, but he thought there would be no further trouble except for possible snipers. His Gurkhas had lost eleven men, with about ninety wounded.

I thanked him, and asked him to have his men chow down as soon as possible. That the planes from the opium fleet to Thailand might return at any time; we needed his men completely concealed in the hangars and warehouses before that happened. I explained that after my Burmese crewmen had towed the wrecked Dove out of sight, our entire fleet would take off for Lashio, and would not return until the Chinese planes on the Vietnamese supply route were back on the field.

Janakpur nodded but looked puzzled. "But, sir, that means we fly back in darkness? There are no lights at Dinjan."

"No, Colonel," I said. "We overnight here and take off for Upper Assam in the morning."

"Righto!" he said, flashed me the flat salute, and was gone again. One by one the planes in our ferry fleet took off empty and banked through the blue sky toward Lashio. When the wrecked Dove had been towed into the first hangar, out of sight, I waggled a thumb at Charley Sunby and Gardella, and our Dakotas fired up and went thundering down and off the Man Hpang runway.

Late in the afternoon we flew back to Man Hpang, the heavier craft following the Doves in. We were not fired on, and when I got out of X-Ray, Colonel Janakpur was waiting. He said that the entire rebel fleet was secured. Nine more of his men had been killed by small-arms fire while taking over the returning planes. I could see at least a score of Chinese corpses littering the edges of the runway, and more on the tarmac before the hangars.

"Fine," I said. "Where is General Pao?"

"This way, please," he said, and I followed him across the field and past the hangar by the operation basha. In its shadow, in the twilight, I saw several disemboweled Chinese. The kukri knives of the Gurkhas had ripped them open.

General Hang Pao was standing in the center of his officers, and he seemed to have been worked over, too. His uniform was ripped, and his face bruised; as I approached he towered over his staff, staring at me bleakly.

"Well, General, we meet again," I said. "This time with no feasts or sword dancers."

He did not deign to reply. From his seven-foot height dark eyes stared over his bruised cheeks, and my head, arrogantly.

I went on. "The last time I was here, General, it cost me a finger. Now it's going to cost you something."

The huge Chinese general did not answer. I turned to Colonel Janakpur. "Take him to the back of the warehouse, where I can speak to him alone. If he balks, put some bayonets in his big ass."

"Righto!" The Gurkha colonel barked an order, and several squadmen pointed toward the back of the warehouse with their naked bayonets. General Pao glanced down at me, hatred in his eyes, and turned to follow them. His massive hands were smoothing at his ripped uniform.

When we were out of earshot of his headquarters staff, I sat down on a bag of rice and lighted a cheroot. When I glanced up, Pao was standing at ease, so I told Colonel Janakpur to feed him a bayonet tip until he felt like coming to attention. It took only two thrusts of the blade before he stiffened.

"Now, General," I said, "you are going to tell me

147

several things about our mutual friend, Captain Pott-schmidt. You are going to tell me where he has gone with the six trunks of rubies and what he has done with Miss LeBlanc. After the rodeo I put on in the Shwe Dagon Pagoda, he can't possibly be still using the room there. So where is he, and what has he done with the Anglo girls?"

Pao did not answer. Colonel Janakpur waved the bloody tip of his bayonet, but I motioned him away.

"All right," I said patiently. "If you do not tell me, tomorrow morning I will have your troops and officers drawn up in formation in the center of the airfield. In full view of all of them, I will have you stand, unbound, and I will mount a box, stool, something, and slap your face. Repeatedly, in front of your men, from side to side, until you tell me what I want to know . . ."

General Pao's eyes flickered. Two thousand years of Mandarin pride might come to grief.

"If I cut your limbs off or savaged you in any way," I continued, "your men might think you were a hero. And I am sure you would endure such things bravely. But if I slap your face long enough, as if you were a common coolie, I think you will never have any face left, any-where. Where are Potts and the girl?"

Sweat was popping out on the broad bronze face. General Pao threw his head around like a gaffed fish, rivulets running down the sides of his nose.

"I will not hurt you," I assured him, "I will only show your soldiers that you can be slapped at will, across the face."

I could hear his teeth grinding.

"If it takes three days, we'll stand out there in the middle of the airfield, where your troops can see how brave their leader is. And if my hands get tired, I will rest them while the latrine coolies are slapping you . . ."

The Mandarins lost; he crumpled. General Pao said that Pottschmidt had kept a suite in the Green Hotel, on the fourth floor in the name of Jamal, since shortly before I had arrived in Rangoon. (Jamal was the seedy cabaret M.C. who had gotten me all the bum information.) The telephone number of the suite, an outside line, was

J-74589, said General Pao; it was the only number he had ever used in contacting Pottschmidt. The rubies were in the suite, but Pottschmidt was planning to move them out of Burma soon. Also, Pottschmidt had told him that if I refused to deal, he would kidnap the girl and deliver her to me a piece at a time. Until I was ready to listen to reason . . .

I considered the big man for a few seconds. Nodded, and Colonel Janakpur and his squad marched the huge Chinese away. Pete Gardella had been sitting off to the side, and he came over to join me.

"You're a mean bastard, pappy," he said, and I held up the barely healed stump of my amputated finger. We walked out of the warehouse, past the silent barracks, and went to Dakota *X-Ray*. I fired up both fans and when the generators were up, I switched on the radio and called Rangoon. Urgent, to General Ne Win.

After I had made the first voice call, the carrier wave hummed on empty air. Then the Rangoon operator broke in and acknowledged, and I asked again for General Ne Win. There was a click, another hum of open wave, and the Burmese dictator's voice said "yes?" as abruptly as usual.

"Captain Mallory reporting, sir. Man Hpang is secured, and all its personnel taken or dead. What do you wish done with the captured troops, planes, and air crews?"

"I told you earlier, Captain. I don't want any trace of them to remain inside Burma." The dictator's voice was crisp. "Burn the planes and installations. Force-march all the personnel across the border to Lantsang, in Yunnan. I will inform the Chinese garrison there that they are coming, through Peking."

"If I could make a suggestion, General . . . Having troops meet General Hang Pao on the Chinese side would be good. But don't you have enough pipeline into Peking to suggest that the actual reception might be made by members of the teen-age Red Guard? It would remove any military protocol to have General Hang greeted by those wild-eyed Maoist dwarfs. They would not much respect his rank."

149

The Burmese dictator laughed. "Captain Mallory, sometimes I suspect you of having an Oriental mind in a barbarian's body. You are right, of course. We will have the young Red Guards welcome Hang Pao back to the land of his ancestors."

"One other thing, sir. It has now become apparent that although General Pao was in command here, the real mover-and-shaker behind the Man Hpang operation is Captain Hal Pottschmidt. Do you know him?"

"I met him several years ago when he was flying for Cathay-Pacific Airways," answered Ne Win.

"Pottschmidt is deeply involved in our problem, General, and he has kidnapped Miss LeBlanc from my suite in the Strand. Only a few minutes ago General Pao told me that he is probably holed up in the rooms registered to Joe Jamal in the Green Hotel. Could you shake the hotel down, sir, and see if Pottschmidt can be taken into custody? And if the girl is being held there, I would appreciate knowing if she is safe."

"We will cordon off the Green Hotel and search it," said the brisk voice. "If Captain Pottschmidt and the girl are inside, we will find them."

"Thank you," I said, and the line clicked. General Ne Win was off the air. No mention of the lost ruby treasure, although he must have known it was gone. I snapped off the set and cut the switches on *X-Ray*. Gardella was looking at me; we were both thinking about the kind of reception General Hang Pao and his Nationalist troops would get.

"Holy Christ!" said Gardella.

"Not involved," I said wearily. "Let's go have that drink now."

Two hours later I received a cable saying that the Jamal quarters in the Green Hotel had been recently and hastily vacated. Neither Pottschmidt, Jamal, nor Solange Le Blanc had been located, but a search was under way. I would be advised. The acid went on gnawing at my belly.

EARLY THE NEXT MORNING I sat in one of the captured jeeps, only a hundred yards from the Sino-Burmese border, and watched an odd footnote to the Asiatic wars reversed with a vengeance. Ground fog was burning away, and on the Chinese side of the border I could see the outskirts of Lantsang; Chinese Communist garrison troops were marching down the fog-wreathed road toward us. They drew up in formation on the other side of the rounded wooden bridge and waited in long ranks of shapeless uniforms which bore no insignia.

Colonel Janakpur was standing beside my jeep; when I nodded, he wheeled and began barking orders to his Gurkha battalion. They herded the remnants of the renegade Nationalist Chinese division down the road and toward the bridge. General Pao was striding ahead of his tatterdemalion troops, towering over his officers.

Pao's long exile was over, but his homecoming would not be auspicious. After seventeen years of commanding a corrupt enclave on Burmese territory he was being ushered into New China. One that had eliminated the fly and the sparrow, and was not likely to cherish late-blooming friends of Chiang.

I tried to locate Harry Liu, my turncoat pilot, as the procession straggled past the jeep, but I did not see him. In a few minutes the renegade division was back on Chinese soil and being herded down the dusty road to Lantsang.

I borrowed Colonel Janakpur's binoculars, and focused them past the rude wooden bridge to the far shore of the river. The Chinese Communist troops stood steady in ranks as their officers directed General Hang Pao's degenerate division. The huge general himself was suddenly attacked and beaten to his knees by a swarm of young zealots in shapeless felt suits. They swarmed over and around him, and his great bulk sank slowly. He was flailing away, an immense Mandarin figure overwhelmed by cuffing and slashing teen-agers. And then he vanished from sight as the only true disciples of the Yenan Caves beat him senseless.

We were back in Man Hpang, and I was ready to take off, with Colonel Janakpur in the copilot's seat, when somebody shouted at me. I leaned out into the aisle and looked back in annoyance. Father MacManus was staggering up through the empty cabin.

"Lad," he called, "you've got to come with me."

"Father, I have important business in Rangoon!"

"I'm sorry about that, lad," he insisted, "but I think you'll have to delay it."

I had been feeling good. Tired, but grimly satisfied. In spite of hell and high water, Pottschmidt, and my other enemies, I had pulled the thing off. And now this perpetually stoned priest wanted to sidetrack me from wrapping up the loose ends.

I cut off both fans and unhooked my belt. Eased out into the aisle. "I hope it won't take long."

"Necessary, Captain," he said, and I followed him through the cabin and back to the ground. We got into a jeep, and he drove it away at high speed toward the Wa village. After the road quit, we had to get out and walk several miles. We passed over the highlands, skirted the swamps, and labored over the rocky outcroppings. Finally we were descending toward the avenue of denuded oaks, stripped but still showing shoots of greenery.

Father MacManus stopped halfway down the avenue of bare trees and pointed toward one of the largest, on our right. My eye ran up it, along the apertures that held embalmed human heads. And I saw it.

One of the heads was not embalmed.

It was the freshly severed head of Solange LeBlanc. She stared out of her rough-hewn niche with tightened mandibles, as if she had been in agony when she died. Her dark hair was in disarray, and her lowered lids seemed to have a fraction of vision left. Her neck had been hacked through unevenly, so that she looked over the Burmese valley from an angle.

I vomited my guts out. Until, finally, I was retching up only a thin, greenish bile. But I could not stop.

"She was put here only a few hours ago," said Father MacManus quietly. "No one saw it done."

When I had heaved awhile longer, he handed me a bottle of Cutty Sark, and I sucked on it, trying to find the bottom. Heat bloomed in my aching gut, and I gave him back the bottle.

"A container, Father," I mumbled. "Something to put it in? Please."

"Right here." He produced an empty cardboard carton, reached up, and removed the severed head. Put it in the carton, and we started jogging up the hillside to the south.

Once I stopped and made him pack the carton with grasses and ferns because the sound of the head rolling around in the carton was too much for me.

W HEN WE RETURNED TO Man Hpang, the installations were burning fiercely, pluming up columns of black smoke. Father MacManus drove the jeep across the busy field, stopped beside *X-Ray,* and I took the paper carton from him, said good-bye, and boarded the plane. Colonel Janakpur was still sitting in the copilot's seat, and I eased in across from him. Scribbling a note on my knee, I handed it back over my shoulder to the radio operator, and heard his key begin chattering.

"General Pao and troops are out of Burma," the

message read, "and Man Hpang installations are burning." Signed, "Mallory."

When it had been sent, I cracked a window and cranked up both fans. The engines checked out, and I let both props idle as Janakpur and I watched my ragtag fleet taking the Gurkha battalion off. The mercenaries would be in Dinjan, in Upper Assam, in time for tiffin, or its Nepalese equivalent.

I was tired to the bone, because it was the most difficult assignment I had ever handled. I should have felt better about it, but the thought of Solange deadened any emotion. Deliberately I shuttered my mind against her image, closed her off. There would be a lot of collective international screaming when the story of the invading civilian battalion was known, but by then it would all be a *fait accompli*.

The Chinese were gone from Burma; the Gurkhas would be back in India, scattered to wherever they had come from before General Singh called them back to battle.

General Singh. That was a big part of the regret I could not escape. He had been a fine old man. The ruby treasure ... I was going to have a sweet few minutes explaining its loss to the Burmese dictator. And the swarthy little man beside me, the Gurkha commander. Where I was going to find over $700,000 in Indian rupees, on short notice, to pay his men off? Plus the two-lakh bonus I had promised. *Somewhere, somehow* ... I thought wearily.

Throttling forward, I was starting to taxi out when a banging began on the side of the plane, a loud metallic din. I braked and looked back down the aisle; motioned for Tin, the copilot, to see what the trouble was. He went back to unlatch the cargo door, and one of Colonel Janakpur's junior officers vaulted into the cabin and came hurrying up toward the pilot's enclosure.

He saluted Janakpur jerkily and handed him a note. The Colonel glanced at it and handed it over to me. While they watched I ripped the flimsy envelope open with my thumb.

"Pappy-san Gall," the note was headed, in Pott-schmidt's tight copperplate scrawl.

> "You always were a hardheaded bastard, and you just kept pushing until it looked like there wouldn't be anything left, after all my years of work. So I had to add another bud to the trees in the Wa forest. Real stupid, Joe; there was enough for both of us, enough for ten people.
>
> Anyway, I'm gone on with the nice collection of king stones and all my running money. You aced me out and are still as honest as the day is long. But the Asian day is getting shorter and darker, Joe. I'll think of you when I count out the pigeon's-blood beauties, and then we'll have to figure out who won.
>
> Faithfully,
> H. Pottschmidt

"Who gave you this note?" I asked the Gurkha lieutenant, and he leaned down and pointed past Janakpur at the planes taking off.

"The big pilot, sir—Captain Potts, your men called him. He is the next one waiting to take off, in the new Dove."

The new Dove. I stared past them, and by God it *was* a new Dove, just turning off the packed red dirt onto the runway, ready to take off.

"Get out!" I said, stabbing a gloved finger at Janakpur, his astonished junior officer, Tin the copilot, and Hla the radio operator. "Out the back, off the plane, *jaldi, jaldi!!*"

They were confused and wanted to argue, but I herded them down through the stripped cabin by main force and, when they had dropped to the ground, slammed and latched the cargo door. Then I went running back to the cockpit, eased into the left seat, and snapped off the brakes. When I poured power to the plane and started rolling across the field with my tail and lifting, Gurkha soldiers scattered ahead of me. I kept applying power because the new Dove was already lifting off, and I had to get *X-Ray* into the air.

T HE DOUGLAS SHUDDERED across the grass with increasing speed as I held everything forward and hauled her off. She tried to settle on me, and I knew if she did, I was gone because I could not keep full power on and retract the gear, too. But I got up a foot, pulling the guts out of her, and then another foot, and was climbing into the twilight.

When I had five hundred feet, I slammed *X-Ray* into a bank to the right, praying that her wings would stay on. The steep bank put me behind the Dove, and as we both fought for altitude I eased the throttles a little. I had the overtaking power and the most machinery.

When Potts saw what he knew so well, that my rate of climb was greater than his, he put the nose of the Dove down and tried violent evasive action. Diving with him, booting the Dakota around like a fighter plane, I jammed my right wing tip under his left one and banked to the left.

That flipped his lighter plane into a spin. The Dove fluttered down through the twilight erratically, and then Potts recovered. Hauled the Dove back into a climb and got over me. I put the throttles back against the panel and went up after him, thinking grimly that my Pratt & Whitney's were far past the red line and had to explode. When they didn't, I rammed up into the bottom of the Dove's fuselage.

Something ripped, and the Dakota started falling away. I heard the left prop of *X-Ray* run away with a tremendous racketing, and tried to feather it. Didn't work; it was windmilling furiously, and I knew that if the prop tips were thrown off, they would come slicing through the cockpit, right at me. Then the right prop quit, and I got it feathered but was sitting in a falling anvil. There was no power on the plane, and I clawed at the cockpit escape hatch.

Potts' Dove was fluttering below me, but he got her leveled off. In the fading light I saw the left cabin door of the Dove break free and go spinning away. Pottschmidt followed it, bailing out. I saw his bulky figure drop, watched his chute pop.

I felt the wind claw into my dead plane as I checked my chute and the belt-holstered kukri Colonel Janakpur had given me. Potts' chute was a pale mushroom receding toward the ground, and I went diving out of the escape hatch toward it.

Plummeting earthward in the dying light, I tried to calculate how far I could free-fall before jerking my chute. Spreading my legs and arms, I got a little planing lift, and snatched the crooked knife from its holster. But even that change of lift lowered my right shoulder, and before I knew it, my head was smashing into the shroud lines of Pottschmidt's chute.

The lines rasped at my face, and I slashed at them. They were nylon, and I was bounced between them, still hacking away. When my stabbing arm met only air, I ripped my own chute, falling away on my back. When it popped, I nearly got my neck broken.

As I swung in increasing arcs, I could see Pottschmidt's chute collapsing below. He was staring up as he plunged out of sight.

After two sickening swings, I smashed down into a rice paddy. The impact was squarely on my bad ankle, and I nearly fainted as the canopy whispered down around me. While I was standing in hip-deep mud hauling the chute off, the indignant Burmese owners of the rice paddy stood on the bank and scolded me properly. *You can lose a lot of rice shoots that way* seemed to be the gist of their comments.

I answered them with some rancor, pointing to my bad ankle. After more scolding they hauled me up onto the bank. And after kyats several had changed hands, they brought a sort of tumbril back, and I was hauled by two unhurried water buffalo to a store with a kerosene lantern glowing inside it. Over the hand-cranked phone I finally shouted my way to a connection with the War Office.

In an hour, through which I sat shaking, encrusted in stinking mud, several Burmese Army vehicles roared down the lane and stopped before the store. I told Major Ba Hla, who was commanding them, approximately where the wreckage of the Dove would be, and he sent me back to Man Hpang in one of the trucks.

Four hours later, as I lay sedated in the Strand Hotel suite with my smashed ankle in a cast, General Ne Win himself called me. Pottschmidt's body had been found by the search teams, and the wreckage of the Dove had been located. The small leather trunks of rubies had been ruptured by the plane's impact, and the gem stones widely dispersed over the area.

"It is thought," the general continued briskly, "that all the jewels will be recovered eventually. The entire crash area is cordoned off by Burmese troops."

"Fine, General," I said. "Good night."

THE NEXT MORNING I was dressed and ready early. The left pant leg of my trousers had been slit to accommodate the cast, and I had finished my packing. In two hours I would be catching the Cathay-Pacific flight to Hong Kong. Colonel Janakpur had been paid. Success breeds many friends, and the delayed currency shipment had arrived suddenly after news of my completed mission had started through the chancelleries of Asia. I had called the U.S. Embassy and demanded the extra bonus lakhs of rupees, and they had been delivered by special messenger in an hour.

Who had held the original fee up? Who knows? Some opportunistic jerks along the agency's pipelines, probably, who were sure that Joe Gall would tap out. Well, he hadn't; he had just been through some unusual strain, and hurt his bad ankle again.

Now, after the fact, Pottschmidt's maniacal rushes to save his opium and contraband empire began to grow clearer. Through some leak in Ne Win's headquarters' staff he had left the Green Hotel in time to avoid capture. Then, with a national warrant out for his arrest, he had sauntered into the Air Burma hangar as cool as he damned, in his flying clothes, and announced that he had joined my team.

His reputation in Asia was so great that no one had thought to question the fact of his employment, and he had commandeered the new Dove. To meet me in Man Hpang by appointment, as he announced jauntily, and all hands had turned to in hastening his departure.

The next step was unclear, but he must have landed at one of the abandoned fighter strips around Rangoon and picked up Solange. And probably the six trunks of rubies. I hope she was dead by then, but I doubt it. His next stop was Man Hpang, and nobody paid any attention to his Dove. Most of us were up at the international border watching General Pao and his bedraggled division going back into Communist China.

The thing to remember is that Potts was thinking, as he landed at Man Hpang, that our fleet had been smashed at Sukrating, and he stepped out into the ruin of all his efforts. Whatever restraint he had left snapped, and he made what must have been a berserk pilgrimage to put Solange's chopped-off head into one of the Wa tree niches. And left the defiant note for me . . . We found her body in the deep shade of the white bamboos.

I hobbled into the sitting room. It looked much as usual except that there was a teakwood coffin on trestles where the big coffee table had been. Inside that tapering box was the torn body of Solange LeBlanc, and I had known her family well. The head had been artfully fitted back onto the body, and she would be flying back to Hong Kong with me. General Win had cleared Solange's coffin through customs, with no prying inspection, and I was grateful to him for that.

"I'll be going now, William," I said, and the little bearer nodded. "Please have the mem-sahib taken downstairs and put into the station wagon."

"Yes, Master." His starched robe rustled as he moved, and I handed him a lot of kyat notes. He did not glance at them, only remarked, "She was a nice lady, master."

"Yes, she was," I said, and went walking out of the suite for the last time. I limped through the whirling silken curtains and went down the hall toward the curving staircase.

When I had crossed the crowded lobby, the tall Sikh doorman said that my station wagon was not available yet. Several cars were blocking the entrance to the hotel loading zone.

"No matter," I said. Rain was sheeting down over Rangoon Town as I stepped out on the sidewalk. The gutters were filling up with rushing brown water, and I went clumping on.

The teak coffin passed me, borne by six laughing chokras. Their splayed feet pattered along the wet sidewalk. *I had never seen Solange when she was not immaculate and cheerful. And the slender girl had been a fast study; she would mispronounce a word once, but always had it right the second time . . .*

Stop that maudlin shit, Sisyphus! I told myself sharply. *She was just one of your people; around you everybody dies. All but you . . .*

I stumped along unhurriedly. Getting drenched, but who cares about an off-duty brigand in the rain? I had been to Burma twice, and that was enough.

Both times, it had been just another penny for the Guy.